A SHATTERED LIFE

A Novel

KAREN SHAPIRO

BQB
North Carolina

Published in the United States by BQB Publishing
(an imprint of Boutique of Quality Books Publishing, Inc.)
www.bqbpublishing.com

Printed in the United States of America

ISBN 978-1-952782-40-4 (p)
ISBN 978-1-952782-41-1 (e)

Library of Congress Control Number: 2021950049

Book design by Robin Krauss, www.bookformatters.com
Cover design by Rebecca Lown, www.rebeccalowndesign.com
First editor: Caleb Guard
Second editor: Andrea Vande Vorde

GAUGER FAMILY TREE

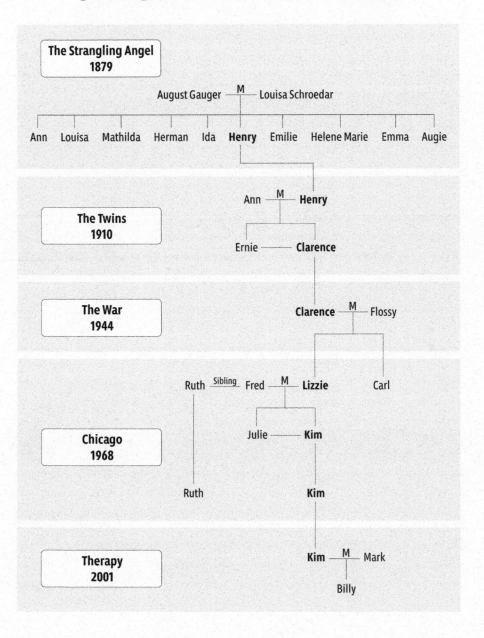

The Strangling Angel
1879

August Gauger ——M—— Louisa Schroedar

Ann Louisa Mathilda Herman Ida **Henry** Emilie Helene Marie Emma Augie

The Twins
1910

Ann ——M—— **Henry**

Ernie ———— **Clarence**

The War
1944

Clarence ——M—— Flossy

Ruth —Sibling— Fred ——M—— **Lizzie**   Carl

Julie ———— **Kim**

Chicago
1968

Ruth   **Kim**

Therapy
2001

Kim ——M—— Mark

Billy

KIM

The lights fade on the oversized screen behind me as I cross the stage, my presentation almost complete. A single cone of white light shines downward onto a podium, and as I enter its orb, the glare of the whiteness blackens my surroundings. I am now in a cocoon, protected and safe, isolated from the auditorium filled with people. Their energy motivates me, encouraging me to continue, but I see only emptiness.

". . . When grief continues to be intense for more than a year, it is complicated grief. It is different than depression and needs an accurate diagnosis so appropriate treatment can be started. Thank you."

The house lights come on and, once again, I see the audience. I hope they find me entertaining as well as informative, but I'm never sure. Years as a psychotherapist have given me confidence, but that experience has yet to cure my performance anxiety. Complicated grief is something I've experienced, but it's easier for me to talk with others about theirs rather than solve the problem within me. I wonder if the audience can see through the smoke and mirrors.

I know my husband, Mark, is sitting out there in the audience. His approval, which was once all I ever needed, is no longer the driver behind my vision. I want the audience's level of energy to validate my effectiveness and success.

When my talk is finished, a few people linger behind to ask additional questions. Out of the corner of my eye, I see Mark move to the far side of the stage where he can observe but remain unseen. He watches me as I interact with each person, taking time to clarify my remarks and comment on any inquiries. Mark tells me I have the grace of a Tai Chi master, the strength of a dancer, and the intellect of an Einstein. He loves me, so he says those things. He sees through my protective façade and understands the deep, horrible pain we both went through with the death of our son. Mark was able to put it aside and move on, while I have continued to sink into a depression that leaves me dead inside.

After everyone leaves, Mark greets me with his usual optimism. "Great job," he says, giving me an obligatory hug. "I know this has been a difficult topic for you, but just the way you presented the material—wow!"

I gather my notes, ignoring his flattery. Turning away, I say, "I hope I had an impact on the audience."

"You are a charismatic speaker," continues Mark. "There were a lot of questions which means you engaged the audience and made them think."

"I don't know," I respond, controlling my agitation. How can he be so overly optimistic? "I don't really know if I got through to anyone."

"You did." Mark looks at his watch. "Let's go back to the hotel."

We are in New York City where I am a guest speaker at a symposium on mental health. Mark took vacation time from his consulting practice to accompany me so we could enjoy a couple of days in the city that never sleeps, even though our idea of a vacation involves a lot of sleep. I don't know if Mark came with me because he wanted the vacation or if his real motive was to be my caretaker in the city where so many conflicting emotions live in my mind. Memories of pain and pleasure, happiness and depression, family and loss are all part of my makeup when I enter New York. I am longing for a balance between these conflicts, but I don't seem to be able to find it.

As we walk along 9th Avenue to the Hudson Hotel, the sidewalks are crammed with people of every ethnic variety, all headed into the maze of New York City. We snake our way through the mix, skirting around the slow walkers and accelerating when trying to beat the walk signs at every corner. At ten p.m. on a weeknight, the city bustles with excitement. Smells waft over us—waves of beer from open-air bars, roasted food from sidewalk vendors, the stale smell of garbage not yet collected are unlike our hometown of Milwaukee.

New York is unique, unlike any other big city. It twinkles at night and never allows silence to enter my mind. The electricity of the city energizes me. The whirling sound of a bicyclist passing, the digital screens illuminating Broadway, and the smell of ethnic food grilling on a food truck all revive good memories. But there are also other memories, painful memories, resurfacing at random moments. Walking in the park with Billy, moving Billy into an apartment, just being with Billy are memories I have buried deep inside, until some sight, some sound, some smell triggers them. The ghosts of New York are with me; I cannot shake their presence.

I wasn't always like this. Mark and I came here long before Billy was born, both of us filled with the joy of anticipating a bright future. It was the jumping-off point of our lives together, as Mark had just taken a position at an actuarial consulting firm and I was an associate professor at our local university. Now I look back and remember the young, idealistic me, confident with the knowledge my life was on the right trajectory.

"Do you want to stop at Maison-Kayser for some dessert?" Mark asks, bringing me back into the present as we reach Columbus Circle.

I hesitate, not sure if I'm in the mood for sweets, although my real concern is whether I want to talk to Mark any further. "Let's just call it a night. I'm tired."

"Okay," Mark says. "Maybe tomorrow we can treat ourselves."

Back at the hotel, I remain silent, lost in thought. I think about my earlier talk at the symposium and look for an honest opinion from Mark. "What did you really think about my speech at the conference?"

Mark's brows knit into a frown and he looks at me through veiled eyes. "I thought you were great. I already told you I knew you were talking from your heart, and you made strong points."

The air becomes so brittle it could snap, or maybe it is me that will snap. Mark's expressions do not sync with his words and the tension it creates surges through me like a low voltage shock. This is our typical conversation—Mark is complimentary but never tells me what he really thinks. I clench my fists in frustration. I'm tired of him placating me when what I really want is to have an honest talk, one where the pain comes out instead of staying hidden. We haven't had a meaningful discussion in years. I brace myself for what's up ahead.

"Mark, stop telling me what you think I want to hear," I say. "I know you're afraid of spending the next three days with me brooding, but you don't have to try and make me feel better to avoid that."

"Kim, that's so far from the truth it's ridiculous," Mark says. His anger rises as he turns away from me and pretends to look for some reading material.

"But that is the truth, and you know it," I retort, circling to face him.

A chilling look edges itself into Mark's face as a storm surges within him. "Whenever I say anything critical, I have to suffer the consequences. So yes, I don't want to say anything." He looks away from me, trying to end what he considers a foolish argument.

I won't let it go. "You were happiest," I blurt out bringing up a long-forgotten issue, "when I gave up my career to take care of Billy. You just don't want to admit it." My voice is loud and terse, my grace faltering.

This time it is Mark who clenches his fists as the volume of his voice rises. "You wanted to stay home and put your career on hold. We agreed. Why are we talking about something from twenty years ago? I can't deal with *your* issues. I'm tired."

"I don't have *issues*. I want your honesty, not pandering."

Mark stiffens his back as he glares at me. "I never stopped you from doing whatever you wanted to do. I knew you would do it anyway. You always do."

"Are you criticizing me for wanting a life of my own? Are you saying I wasn't a good mother? I protected Billy as best I could." I storm off into the bathroom to brush my teeth, anything to get away from Mark.

"Dammit, don't ignore me," Mark demands. "You always start these arguments and then leave when I don't agree with you. And this has nothing to do with you being a good mother."

I am shaking with anger. "But you blame me. Every time. Our life together is meaningless. We are going through the motions of the happily married couple, but we aren't."

The piercing ring of a phone interrupts our argument. Mark answers, is silent for a moment, and says, "Sorry, no problem."

"Who's calling?" I ask.

He shakes his head in shame. "We're making too much noise and the people next door can't sleep."

"It's only eleven o'clock. I thought this was the city that

never sleeps. Whatever." I slam the bathroom door and am alone.

I take a couple of deep breaths and look at myself in the mirror. Anger is not a pretty sight on my face. My eyebrows bump together, my nose widens, my lips press into a thin line, and the fine lines around my eyes are now deep crevasses. I never meant for the argument to happen, but now the words are out, and I am afraid of the consequences.

I cannot look in the mirror any longer, so I step into the shower and turn the shiny chrome dial to let the hot water flow over me in an everlasting waterfall. The steam calms me, and rivulets of water drip down my side as my mind begins to slow down. I want to stay under its healing magic forever.

The next few days, Mark and I pretend like the argument never happened. We treat each other with extreme politeness. We do all the New York things we like: a play, a walk through the village, dinner at fabulous restaurants, all totally normal New York things to do. We are once again the couple that has it all. The mask is in place.

Once home in Milwaukee, we settle into our normal pattern of living, except nothing is normal. Going out to eat, we argue about which exit to take off the expressway. When we get to a restaurant, we argue about where to park the car. When ordering food, we cannot reach an agreement on whether to share our dinners or order separately. Tension fills our lives every day. Sometimes simply being in the same room provokes an argument.

I think back to the early days of our marriage and the passion Mark and I felt. We would be at parties and steal away into the bathroom for "a quickie," or take a long lunch and just smile at each other, holding hands under the table. He was the only drug I ever needed.

Our life started out like a fairy tale. All I ever wanted from Mark was kisses, hugs, and the smile in his eyes. His long, dark curly hair attracted me from the beginning, although he told me later, he only grew his hair long to counteract the nerd image he had being a math major. He was muscular, clean-shaven, and his casual dress betrayed the conservative businessman within.

Everything about him was soft with an understated joy. He filled me with happiness.

We both had successful careers, a house in the suburbs, and, eventually, a son. Outwardly, we had the perfect marriage, the perfect family, and the perfect life. It's too bad it took so much effort to create the image, and even more to maintain it. Nobody knows what is revealed once the surface is scratched. The loss of our son propelled me to make meaning out of my pain. I did the only thing that made sense, and the next thing I knew I was giving talks on grief. I don't see Mark grieving like I do, so I can't help but feel isolated in my own pain.

Divorce is not an option for me, as Mark is the only person I ever wanted. Our issues are not about love, because I can never love anyone else, but about making our relationship feel right. What I want is to find a way to get past our now-established barrier of non-communication and put our broken pieces back together. It is not an easy job.

"What do you want for dinner tonight?" I ask.

"Do you want to go out to the Bistro?" Mark responds.

"Sure," I say. "What time?"

"I have a little work first, so how about six p.m.?"

"Sounds good," I say.

We finish our work and get to the restaurant in time to watch the young bar crowd milling around, trying to impress one another. Once seated, we order our food and stare at other people because we are unable to make conversation with each other.

"How was your day today?" I ask, trying to make conversation.

"It was boring. Nothing really going on. No new mergers in the insurance industry." Mark says as he sips his glass of wine. "How was your day?"

"Kind of the same. I had one interesting patient who thinks the world is coming to an end because we don't have a female president, and she wants me to fix it," I respond with the same lack of enthusiasm. "I think I need to take some time off."

"You do work hard," Mark says, looking away from me.

I sigh. "I know when we were in New York last month I felt really anxious. I always get nervous before a presentation, but the nervousness lasted a long time. Maybe New York does strange things to me."

"Probably," Mark says, staring at a spot on the table.

Our food arrives, and we put aside thoughts of New York, both of us wordlessly sharing the same sorrow of that city. Neither the savory pasta marinara nor the linguine with clams, not to mention a bottle of red wine, can penetrate our mood or remove the communication barrier between us. Boredom sets in. It is an invitation for my brain to find a new path out of this tedium.

Gazing at the bar once again, I see the patrons talking and laughing. Their energy floats around the room, and I sense their joy, a feeling I seem to lack. My life is missing that joy. Playtime used to involve Mark and Billy, but sadness has intervened and pushed everybody away. Mark was always the light of my life. I know his peace, but it is so distant now I don't know how I could ever find a way back to him.

Once home, I go upstairs to take a shower to relax. An

evening shower prepares me for sleep and quiets my mind, just the opposite of the many people who use a shower to wake them up. I look at my image in the mirror and the reflection shows the aging process at work. My skin is less elastic and mottled, making it look thick. My makeup has worn off, which leaves my skin with a pale texture of veins running across my cheeks like connected rivers. The red bumps of rosacea, now fully visible, look like teenage acne, only I will not grow out of it.

My skin is dry and itchy. I look at my profile and think I have lost weight, usually a welcome happening, but now I look like I'm imploding into myself, with my posture compromised. I step into the shower and the hot water is soothing, masking many of my concerns. I stand there for several minutes, relaxed and calm. I begin to wash myself but stop when I feel a bulge in my armpit. I decide to go a day without shaving them, so I continue to lavish in the luxury of my shower.

Drying off with the soft, fluffy spa towel, I again feel the lump. Once more I look at myself in the mirror, raise my hands high above my head, and see a large protrusion in my armpit. This can't be good.

"Mark!"

ROUND ONE

"**A**ngioimmunoblastic T-Cell Lymphoma," says Dr. Belmont.

"What?" I respond.

"The pathologist diagnosed your cancer as Angioimmunoblastic T-Cell Lymphoma."

"What the hell is that?"

Focusing his gaze directly on me, Dr. Belmont wants to be sure I understand. "The Cleveland Clinic diagnosed the type of Lymphoma you have. We wanted to be sure the treatment protocol was correct."

Stunned into silence, I feel resentful toward Dr. Belmont, who is calmly sitting at his desk, wearing his white doctor's coat, and delivering devastating news. He's speaking in brief, unhurried sentences, as if talking to a person who can't understand complicated information. He reminds me of an anchorman, whose only mission is to deliver succinct soundbites.

"Why did it take two weeks to make this diagnosis?" I ask defiantly.

"Your condition is unusual," says the doctor.

"So, what did the Cleveland Clinic have to say?" My mouth becomes dry as I set my jaw into a rigid line.

Pushing his overly large, tortoise-shell glasses onto his nose, Dr. Belmont continues. "T-cell Lymphoma is more aggressive than B-Cell. We have to look at different treatment options."

"So, I'm the lucky one who got the incurable form of Lymphoma?"

"No, it's not incurable." Dr. Belmont remains calm and shows little affect, not even sympathy. "You will need chemotherapy . . . in your case, it's called CHOP."

Inhaling deeply and breathing out slowly, I ask with a shaky voice, "What am I facing?"

In a professional manner, Dr. Belmont begins. "You will receive four different chemo drugs in one day as an infusion, followed by three weeks off. The drugs are strong and should kill the bad cells. The side effect of the drugs will likely include fatigue, nausea, hair loss . . ."

"Stop!" I yell, interrupting his monologue. "Am I going to die? Every day I feel worse, and now I have some rare, aggressive disease."

"I understand what you're saying," responds the affectless Dr. Belmont. "None of this is easy, and there's a lot of uncertainty that can't be avoided."

Mark places a hand on my arm trying to quiet my agitated nerves, but I pull away, rebuffing his attempt at soothing me. I want my anger. I want Mark to leave me alone to handle it. So much feels out of my control, having my own anger feels empowering.

Controlling the taut tone of my voice, I ask, "What is the prognosis?"

"It's uncertain at this time," replies Dr. Belmont. "There are a lot of factors going into the success of this treatment."

"Uncertain?" I look at Mark. He is outwardly calm, but a distant calm. There are signs of anxiety he is cleverly masking. I can see it in the creases around his mouth and the slight tremor around his eyes. I know him so well. Tears well up in my eyes as the world begins to shrink away from me, replaced by a cold void.

"Tell me about the uncertainty," Mark interjects. "What are we looking at?"

Relieved to be talking to Mark rather than me, Dr. Belmont explains. "There will be six rounds of chemotherapy with three weeks between each session."

"What is the prognosis?" Mark asks the question again, already having heard the answer once. Maybe he thinks if he asks it over and over, he will get the answer he wants.

"It's difficult to say," Dr. Belmont patiently replies. "Every case is different. This is a rare form of Lymphoma and not a lot of research is available. Mortality rates are higher."

This is not the answer Mark is looking for, but he doesn't press any further. He always does this, pretending he's already accepted it all.

It is suffocating in this closed, cramped office. Mark and Dr. Belmont continue to talk while I slip into a coma-like state.

When the weight of the pressure becomes unbearable, I break out of my void. "When the chemo is over, what is my quality of life?"

Dr. Belmont stares at me, losing his patient demeanor. "Again, each case is different, but you are starting out healthy and have no other medical conditions to interfere with the treatment."

"You can't give me a better answer?" I challenge him. "Have you ever *heard* of this thing I have?"

Mark interrupts before I can go any further. "This diagnosis is a shock to both of us, so please understand our reluctance to accept it."

"I don't want a wig," I blurt out, inadvertently grabbing my hair and running my fingers through the blonde curls that will soon be gone.

Dr. Belmont and Mark both stare at me, and I realize how foolish I sound. My mind is gray and fuzzy, like a fog where the sun is unable to break through the iron curtain of clouds. I know the seriousness of this diagnosis, but my thoughts are erratic.

"Don't worry about your hair now," Mark says, admonishing me. "The important thing is to get you well."

"I want to get well, but I don't want to lose myself in the process," I say, such a simple desire.

Dr. Belmont sees the tension building, and with calm indifference, he says, "You can start the chemo treatment next Monday. Get plenty of rest over the weekend."

The meeting is over, and uncertainty hangs in the air. As Mark and I leave the doctor's office, I move slowly, like an injured puppy. Mark's gravity-drawn shoulders belie any feeling of optimism, and his sad eyes focus on a distant point, away from me. We are alone with our thoughts, separated by an invisible wall. Will it ever be dismantled?

━━━◆━━━

Monday morning, Mark and I arrive at the cancer center, ready to face the first round of treatment. Unexpectedly, a Zen-like atmosphere greets us, and a faint odor of jasmine permeates the air that was designed to create a garden-like feel. We enter a habitat where mental health and physical well-being intertwine. Every surface is dust-free, and bamboo palms and fiddle-leaf figs fill every corner with life-giving energy. The minimalist décor is serene.

"Are you okay?" Mark asks me.

"It's now or never," I answer, not wanting to think about what lies ahead.

We approach the sleek, wood-and-metal-framed reception desk, and Mark begins speaking. "This is Kim Weber," he says. "We are here for her first chemo session."

The receptionist smiles with friendly, welcoming eyes, and I force a limited smile onto my face. My mouth moves into a subtle *U* shape, but everything else remains fixed in a stoic stare.

Once Mark fills out the forms, I take my place along a wall of windows, populated with at least ten large reclining chairs facing Lake Michigan. A curtain separates each space, and other patients are receiving their treatments as they gaze out the window and enjoy the scenery. The nurses interact in a friendly manner, giving out medical information and discussing the weather. The patients easily exchange pleasantries and seem able to ignore the needles poking into their veins.

I turn to Mark and say, "You know, you don't have to stay. It's going to take about three hours."

"Of course I'll stay. Do you think I would leave you alone on your first chemo session?"

"I will probably read my emails while I get treatment. I brought my computer. You really don't have to stay. I'm fine."

"Kim, you know I'm staying."

"Suit yourself." I look outside at the view and realize my old office is just around the corner. "Did you notice this is the same view of the park and Lake Michigan I had from my old office? I can reminisce about better times."

He knows that when I mention better times, I mean the times when Billy was a boy, before we knew the heavy grief that replaces him in every room.

Mark looks at me with compassion. "Don't get discouraged," he says. "You're an incredibly strong person, and I know you will beat this."

"Sure," I say, trying to sound positive. "At least the view is good."

The reclining chemo chair is like a Barcalounger, the kind my grandpa always fell asleep in while watching TV. It's for old people, but looking around, I realize I am now a member of that group. A nurse comes over to cover me with a heated blanket, which radiates warmth and feels good against my skin. I try taking deep breaths to meditate, but unfortunately, even after twenty years of yoga, mindful meditation still alludes me. The nurse arranges the tubes descending from the bags of drugs and inserts a needle into my vein. Time to start.

The drips start, and my frail hands begin to shake. The window's glass reflects my image, and my eyes examine the surface of my face. My skin is ashen, my usually full cheeks have sunken into the hollows of my facial skeleton, and my eyes, lips, nose, and eyebrows have flattened into a plane with little texture. The sickness has taken its toll.

I wrap my fingers around the gold coin in my hand and squeeze the good luck charm given to me by my mother years ago. The feel of the fine lines forming the face of lady liberty and its golden reflection help to ease my fear of the treatment.

The chemo nurse quietly appears from behind the privacy screen and sees me clenching my fists. "You're cutting off all of the circulation to your fingers. What are you squeezing so tight?"

Surprised by this interruption, I tell her my story. "It's a gold coin my great-grandfather brought home from the War Between the States, or so the story goes. It glows in the sunlight and I hope it will bring me luck."

"I'm sure it will," replies the nurse. "How did you end up with it? A coin that old and solid gold is pretty valuable."

"It probably is, but I'll never sell it. My mother gave it to me before she died, and she got it from her father. I'm not sure how he got it, but he gave it to my mom on the day she married my father. I don't know the mystery, only the meaning."

"That's a romantic story," says the nurse as she switches the chemo bags, making sure I get the right stuff.

"I question how lucky that was, after all, she had to live with my father. I'm not sure that turned out to be lucky!" I laugh despite myself, thinking back to my days as a child living with an angry parent. The nurse finishes regulating my chemo drips and leaves to treat her other patients.

"I appreciate your sense of humor," Mark says. "At least you can laugh about your family crises."

I think back to the day my mother gave me the coin. She knew she did not have long to live and was suffering terribly with her cancer. This was before the days of chemotherapy when radiation was the standard treatment. It didn't work for my mother, and she slowly, painfully faded away. "Kim," she said one day after a particularly difficult radiation treatment. "I want you to have something dear to me."

"You already gave me everything I need," I replied. "I don't need a good luck charm. I've had sixteen years with you."

"This is not a lucky charm, but more of a legacy. It has been in our family for a long time, and I want it to stay there for generations to come. You should be the keeper of memories."

My mother's eyes became tearful as she placed the gold coin in my hand.

"Are you sure I'm that person?" I asked. "You know what a scatterbrain I can be."

"You will grow out of that phase of your life. I see you in a different light and I know you are the person to keep this legacy."

My mother closed her eyes, having been exhausted by our conversation.

I looked at her with sadness, knowing our time together was limited. I choked back tears and said, "I am honored."

It was a week after this conversation that my mother passed. I was young and foolish at the time, but I never forgot the importance of the coin. It was a link between me and all who came before me, and it carried their untold stories. I could make as much luck out of it as I wanted. Now I wonder if all this time it has only carried misfortune. If I'm cursed.

As the chemo treatment progresses, I begin to unwind and think about my mother and her final days of cancer. After a while, the nurse reappears to check on my treatment. "I see your hands are looser now. The coin must have worked its magic," she says with optimism.

"I guess. I'd like to believe it can get me through this ordeal with a little dignity left."

"You're strong, you'll do fine," she says as she smiles and tucks some more warm blankets around me.

Turning to Mark, who is working on his computer, I say, "I apologize for my earlier outbursts. I'm working on becoming more positive."

Mark nods but doesn't look away from his screen. Finally, he looks at me and says, "I wonder if we'll see Dr. Belmont today."

"I hope not. He is so unsympathetic it makes my blood boil. He talks like a robot spewing pre-programmed soundbites."

"I admit he has the attitude of someone excessively proud of himself," says Mark. "I didn't like him either."

Time passes slowly and I cannot focus on the magazine I am trying to read. Mark is back to his computer, engrossed in some transaction reports about the latest merger or acquisition deal, or something like that. I gaze out of the window to see what is happening outside and quietly slip into a fantasy world where cancer does not exist. My chair looks out over a park with Lake Michigan as a backdrop. The ambiance is peaceful, no ice floes or turbulent movements. The park along the shoreline is alive with people enjoying the outdoors, wrapped in woolen scarves, hats, and mittens. Below my window, a bike path transports riders to the downtown area. Everybody looks happy and free, something I no longer feel.

Mark sees me staring out the window. "What's going on out there?" he asks. "Did you get this distracted by the view when you were working in the beautiful Victorian mansion just down the street?"

I think back to the days when I maintained a private office for my Psychotherapy practice. "I did not get distracted when I was really concentrating, or working with a difficult patient," I recall. "But my clients found it a peaceful place. I wish those serene vibes would sink into me now."

"Don't worry," Mark says. "You will get through this episode of your life, and we will get back to normal."

"You look at things differently. I'm not sure I even know what normal is. Are we a normal couple? Do normal people act like we do when cancer strikes?" I look away and try to focus on the blue winter sky, now dotted with multiple hues of white fluffy clouds. I have too many feelings of grief related to Billy's absence. Now is no time to bring it up. Concentration is difficult, and for the first time in several days I want to talk openly about my cancer.

"Mark," I say taking his attention away from his computer.

"I am fighting a battle where the enemy is smart and has a lot of complexity."

Closing his computer, Mark answers, "I know this is difficult, but you will get through it. I know you will."

"Thanks, but you're not the one with a needle in your arm. This disease is dangerous and more flexible than I am. It can change with everything I throw at it, and it often wins. I feel like I'm fighting a monster."

The logic which is so much a part of Mark's makeup disintegrates, and he closes his eyes to stop the tears from forming. His feelings are usually invisible, but he can no longer hide his emotions. "Kim," he says, turning to look into my clouded eyes. "We need to face this together and be a team. We cannot only fight with chemicals but also use the power of our wills. We are winners and we'll show it. I love you."

"Please just listen to me, and don't tell me everything will be all right." My throat tightens as my mouth dries, making speech difficult. I steady myself and say, "I may not want to fight this monster. I may want it to win. I can't face a useless life, and if that's what is in front of me, I'd rather pass away now, quietly."

A nurse interrupts this private moment to ask how the treatment is going.

"Fine," I say, angry at the interruption.

"The anti-nausea medication and most of the chemo drugs are finished." She seems so proud of me. "You're almost done."

When the nurse walks away, Mark addresses me, and instead of the compassion I expect, he is almost purple with rage. "What are you saying? You've accepted defeat? You have never been one to give up on anything in your entire life, including me. You are a fighter, and sometimes you piss me off so much I actually want you to go away, but not now, not with this. You can't give up. I won't hear of it, and I don't want you to ever say it again."

"You're not the one fighting this beast," I counter. "You're not the one who can't go out and do normal things, and you're not the one suffering."

Mark lowers his voice, afraid of being overheard. "You're right, I'm not the sick one here, but I am the one who is going to push you to your limits to keep you going. I will not tolerate anything less from you."

"We'll see," I say. I look at the needle in my arm. "But some things can't be changed. I'll never be able to resume a normal life, as if we had one. Isn't it better to have faith in the natural process of birth, life, and ultimately, death?"

"No, it is not." Mark is adamant. "We have science to interrupt the natural order of life, and that is what you are going to do. Use science. I will make sure you do."

The natural order of death. Is that how he has come to see Billy's passing? Just a part of the natural order?

Shortly after this conversation ends and the silence in the air is almost unbearable, the nurse returns wearing a protective gown that looks like a hazmat suit. "We're ready for the red drug," she says cheerfully.

I don't feel cheerful, and her suit looks ridiculous. "You look like you're going to the Medical Prom but can't afford a new dress. Why do you need protective gear?"

"It's just a safety precaution. This particular drug is harmful if it gets on your skin or clothing."

I frown.

"I know," the nurse says. "It sounds worse than it actually is. I'm just being careful. Besides, I don't care if I ruin this prom dress."

Another half hour and the chemo treatment is over. I leave

the hospital with slow, unsteady steps and make my way to our car. Mark offers to help, but I brush him away, not wanting any assistance.

The chemicals have already affected my bodily functions. My gait is slow, almost robotic, as I struggle to put one foot in front of the other. Even though the treatment was not physically painful, I am tired and need to rest. Emotional pain wracks my body and I feel powerless.

Once home, I wrap myself in my favorite cozy blanket and try to relax. The pre-cancer version of me was brave, but this new facsimile of what I once was is scared, worried, and withdrawn. I am afraid of everything. "Can I get you anything?" Mark asks, sensing my fears.

"No," I quietly answer. "I just need to rest and let the drugs do their magic."

"I'll be here if you need me," Mark says.

That evening, I try to watch television, but my emotions trap me in uncertainty and demand attention. I am afraid of becoming nauseous, so I do not eat. I worry about developing mouth sores, so I do not talk. I constantly wash my hands because I worry about infection. But most of all, I worry about being isolated from everyone I love.

The next day, the mailman delivers a welcome gift from my sister Julie. She compiled years of genealogy research and turned it into a scrapbook of our family history all the way back to the 1870's. Julie put a note inside the cover telling me to prepare myself for an eye-popping read. We have notorious events and scandals in our family.

I don't know if reading events from decades ago will be fun or eye-popping, but I welcome the distraction. I have questions about the origins of my cancer, and this may give me some answers to the medical mystery of why I got Lymphoma. I know our bodies can be predisposed to some illnesses, but I do not know if Lymphoma is one of them. Maybe I have an epigenetic alteration in my DNA.

Initially, I page through the scrapbook quickly and see pictures of Julie and me, Mark and Billy, my parents, Lizzie and Fred, and my grandparents, Clarence and Flossy. There are older prints of people I don't recognize but are somehow connected to this sprawling family tree.

One picture catches my attention. It is a sepia-toned, cracked, distressed photo of a family standing in front of an old farmhouse; my sister titled it, "The Gaugers, late 1870s." I assume the people in it are a husband and wife with their eleven children. The edges of the photograph are damaged and a large crease cuts diagonally through the family. The girls all wear black jacket-bodice tops with floor-length skirts dragging on the ground. The boys are in knee-length knickers and shirts in dark, plaid colors. Most are barefoot, no one is smiling. One of the boys does not conform and stares away from the camera with squinting eyes and a mouth turned down at the corners.

There's always a maverick in the crowd, I think, identifying with the little boy who refuses to be like the others. He looks strong with a determined face and posture, and an expression of defiance. He distances himself from his sisters and seems as if he doesn't want to be there. Is he a loner or just angry? Am I like the boy in the picture? Do I have determination, individually, independence? My brain is getting lost in the fantasy, I better stick to the facts I know.

Even though color photography wasn't available at the time of this photo, I can see this family has blond hair and blue eyes just like me. They are tall, and the similarities in physical appearance make me think I am a direct descendent of someone in this picture. I'd like to know more.

I remember Julie mentioning the Gauger name as part of our ancestral tree. They were German immigrants and farmers in the late 1800s. Could they have passed a Lymphoma gene on to me? I doubt if records were kept that long ago, but it would be interesting to know. Maybe my gold coin came from this family? They look too poor to have anything of value like gold coins, but maybe paper currency hadn't reached them as yet.

Turning to the next page, I find a newspaper article titled, "Diphtheria Strikes Brandon." The date at the top of the page is June 12, 1879, and the article describes an epidemic sweeping through the farming community. Nobody knows where it came from, but fatalities are high. I flip back to the previous page and look at the children of the Gauger family, their demeanor so serious, unlike photos of today. How many of these children survived the epidemic? Which one, if any, do I descend from?

I close the scrapbook and rest my eyes for a moment. Looking at pictures from the past gives me the peace of knowing that life continues in the hearts and minds of family. These old photos stir my imagination and I drift off thinking of the little boy with the scowl on his face, wondering what he was like. I wake suddenly as the scrapbook slips off my lap and falls to the floor with a clatter. As I pick it up, I also grab the envelope it came in and another, smaller, older book drops out.

This book is simple, an earthy hued cover and a sweet, musky smell. The worn pages are fragile with edges soft to the touch, like a well-loved teddy bear. On the cover is a sticky note from Julie that says "Clarence's Diary."

It takes a second or two for the information to sink in, but once it does, I forget my early fatigue and my lips stretch into a wide grin. A buzz of electricity goes through my brain as I realize this diary is the gift I need to plow ahead. I may not get all the answers I seek, but I will know where to start.

I remember my grandfather, Clarence. He was a flamboyant politician and newspaper man whom my mother admired greatly. I tentatively open the diary to a random page and read an entry about his life on a farm and how much he dislikes it. I backtrack to earlier pages, and read about conflicts Clarence had with his father, Henry. This information is all new to me and exciting. I now have the name and some information all the way back to my great-grandfather. It's a start.

Henry is my great-grandfather. I wonder if the boy in the picture is him.

THE GAUGERS

THE STRANGLING ANGEL

HENRY
SUMMER 2009

W hen I first felt sick, my parents hoped it was an ordinary
sore throat and headache, but when I couldn't swallow
and the fever hit, they knew it was serious. Our country
doctor was in Waupun, only ten miles away, but my brother,
Herman, had to ride there on our old horse, Buck, and it was a
slow journey. As much as Herman tried to coax Buck to move
faster, it took a long time to get to the doctor, and my breathing
was becoming more and more labored.

I have no clear memory of what happened, but I do remember
my body going from drenching sweats to relentless shivers,
making my muscles ache and clouding my already frazzled
mind. My breathing was raspy, and I was in serious pain. I
saw the anxious look on my mother's face, pale and terrified,
fearing the outcome of whatever imminent danger awaited me.
The rest of my family kept their distance, as my father would
not let anyone close for fear of my unknown condition.

At nine years old, I was the sixth of eleven children to August
and Louisa Gauger. We lived on a ten-acre farm near Brandon,
Wisconsin, where we raised cows and chickens along with a
multitude of dogs, cats, and any other animals wandering onto
our land. Recently, we had added more cows to our herd so we
could produce and deliver milk to the nearby Hazen Factory,
built by Charles Hazen solely to produce cheese. Prior to that,

cheese-making was considered women's work, done at home. Brick cheese was now made in a factory, and I liked that because it brought in needed extra money.

My life on the farm was enjoyable despite the rigorous physical demands required to make a living off the land. During harvest season, my dad would let me ride on the horse-drawn grain harvester he'd recently purchased in Beloit from the Deering Manufacturing Company. They invented a reaper to incorporate a twine binder and automate the operation of bailing hay. I was proud that my father was always on top of the latest developments, which made us proficient at getting our crops to market. One day I would own the farm and follow in my father's footsteps.

Our neighbors were a short distance away, and after my chores were complete, I would walk over to their farm to play with my best friend, Charlie. He also came from a big family, so to avoid the other kids, we would hide in the hayloft. We pretended the bales of hay were stonewalls when we played army, mountains when we played cowboys and Indians, and massive trees when we were explorers in an unknown world.

One afternoon, as I approached the farm, I could see Charlie's parents building a bonfire by throwing toys and clothing into the flames. "What are they doing?" I thought. "Those toys could be fun, and Charlie and I can still play with them."

A shirt dropped from their pile of clothes, and I picked it up and brought it to Charlie's mother. "Get away from here and stay out of our house!" she screamed as she grabbed the shirt away from me and threw it into the fire.

"But I want to see Charlie." Shocked by her outrage, I could not understand why she wanted me to leave. I thought she liked me.

Confused, I ran home through the corn field and rushed

into my house where I crumpled to the floor. My mother was preparing dinner, and when I told her about the way Charlie's mom yelled at me, a look of dread passed over her face and she, too, started to yell. "Did you touch anything?" Angry tears formed in the corner of her eyes, turning them liquid and fearful.

"No. I don't understand why they are throwing away perfectly good things."

"There is sickness in their house, and we must protect ourselves by staying away. I don't want you playing with Charlie until this danger passes."

"Why not?" I said, challenging my mother. "Charlie is my best friend, and we're building a fort in his hay loft. We need to finish it before the next harvest."

My mother softened her gaze and relaxed, touching my shoulder. "Charlie's little sister, Emma, just died of diphtheria. Being around her is dangerous. We don't know how she got sick, but it can strike anyone, especially young children. I don't want you bringing it into our house. Stay away from Charlie and his family for now."

My mother hugged me and murmured about being safe and keeping the evil winds away. I still did not understand but thought I should reassure her I was safe and would not play with Charlie until she said I could. I didn't believe in evil winds and could not imagine anything bad being at Charlie's house, so I was sure I was completely safe.

"What is diphtheria?" I asked.

"It is an evil sickness that keeps you from breathing."

Four days later I became sick, my mother unable to protect me. It started with a sore throat and fever, and by the end of the day, my labored breathing became painful. Our family doctor prescribed whiskey to try to clear the membrane forming inside my windpipe. He said it would help keep the air passage clear, but recommended I see a special doctor to treat the disease.

The following morning, I was worse. The special doctor was making rounds near us, and my parents brought him to our house to treat me. I tried to focus on what he was saying, but I was in pain and kept drifting in and out of consciousness. I couldn't concentrate enough to listen to him, but I did hear things like "infection has progressed," "little can be done," and "experimental tracheostomy." My mother was crying, begging him to try something, but before he responded, I fell into blackness.

When I awoke, the doctor and my parents were still whispering in hushed tones. Their grim faces sent waves of hopelessness through me and a tightness formed in the pit of my stomach. When that tightness reached my throat, I felt fire and tried to scream but no sound came out. Something was in my throat and the pain it caused stopped all air from passing. I was terrified.

I remained still and strained to listen to the doctor talking to my mother. "We are not out of the woods yet," he said, his voice trembling. "There is a high risk of infection around the tracheostomy tube and isolation from the other children is absolutely necessary. Nobody knows exactly how this disease is spread, but diphtheria tends to strike families, especially younger children. Keep Henry away from the others."

The following week, an uneasy pattern of wakefulness and deep sleep kept me in a fog, and I could not understand what was happening. I was hungry, but it was so painful to eat or drink that I avoided food and only ate when my mother forced me to swallow mere tablespoons of water or broth. Anything solid sent piercing pain down my throat. Every day, she cleaned and dressed the wound in my neck. I wondered if I was going to have to spend the rest of my life with a tube sticking out of my neck. Talking was impossible, but I was able to breathe.

The progress was slow, but gradually I improved and became aware of what was going on around me. I hadn't seen any of my siblings in over a week, and I had no idea what was happening on the farm. Did somebody do my chores for me? I bet they were mad, especially my older brother, who always complained I never did enough work. The fort Charlie and I were building in his barn had probably been taken over by *his* brother, who always wanted to play with us.

My mother told me the special doctor was coming soon to see me and check on my progress. I really didn't want to see him again, but my mother said it was necessary to remove the tube so I could get better.

I tried to speak, but it took so much effort to push the air out of my lungs, my vocal cords were useless. I managed to create a weak, gruff sound as I pointed to my throat, but pain prevented any real words from forming.

My mother saw me struggling. "Do you want to know what happened to your throat?"

I nodded.

Slowly, my mother described the procedure with the precision of a trained nurse and a calmness I didn't know she possessed. "The doctor started the surgery without medicine to make you sleep. You were already unconscious. He used only a few tools from his pocket instrument case, a scalpel and a tracheostomy tube. I boiled the water for him so he could sterilize and make everything free of germs. The only light we had available, besides that window over on the wall, was a kerosene lamp that your father held over the bed. I tried to assist wherever I could, but I was so scared I could not offer much help."

My brain stuttered for a moment while I tried to understand what my mother was telling me. *I had surgery and that is why I can't talk. Was this real or is my brain so messed up I can't understand?*

"You had diphtheria," my mother continued with the same measured calmness. "It's serious because a membrane grows over your breathing tube and eventually stops you from breathing. The doctor made a cut in your throat where the infectious membrane was growing." My mother pointed to her throat as I touched the tube in mine.

"That's right," she nodded. "The doctor inserted the tube into the cut. He had to suck out the choking membrane, but as soon as that happened, darling, I could see your breathing was easier. The blueish color of your face became flush again. I wanted to squeeze you as tight as I could, I was so overjoyed, but you were unconscious, and I was afraid I might hurt you." The love in my mother's voice was strong, but the longer she talked, the more distraught she became.

"This was good news, wasn't it?" Something was not right. My mother should be happy, but she looked upset.

My mother recovered her composure. "Of course, it's good news; I just need to relax. I love you."

A few days later, the special doctor came back to our farm to check on my progress. "Henry is my first success with this method of treatment. You did a good job keeping the wound clean and no infection set in. Very few children ever recover from this illness."

"Will he survive?" my mother asked.

"I think so. I need to remove the tube, and we will see if he can breathe on his own. At least this time I have an anesthetic with me."

Focusing on the doctor, I tried to pay attention to the

instructions he gave my mother, but they spoke in low, mumbled tones. I felt they were keeping secrets from me, maybe things I should not know or something that would scare me. The doctor poured a liquid into a cloth and approached me. He said something about being asleep, or maybe it was my sister, Ida, who was asleep, but I could sense something was wrong and my body stiffened in anticipation.

The doctor moved the cloth toward me, and my hands flew to my face for protection. Without thinking, I yelled at my mother, not caring about the stabbing pain in my throat. I smelled something sweet, like paint remover, and thought of the afternoon my father and I had painted our barn door. That image quickly vanished, and I struggled to push the cloth away, but soon everything became black, and I sank into the void.

When I awoke, I was alone in the bedroom I shared with my older brother. My head hurt, my throat was on fire, but my breathing seemed almost normal. Touching my throat, I felt a large cloth covering my neck, but the tube was gone. Could I be breathing on my own? I swallowed and still felt pain, but I was able to breathe. Maybe I was going to live after all.

I stayed motionless for a while, dozing periodically, until my mother came in to check on me. She didn't look happy. Maybe I was wrong in thinking my breathing was normal, and this was only a brief reprieve before my body succumbed to the strangling angel.

"How are you feeling?" my mother asked.

Struggling through the pain of talking, I pointed to my bandages.

"My throat hurts." I was barely able to form the words.

"You have been asleep for a long time, but the doctor said you are doing well."

After another silence, my tearful mother composed herself

and said, "Ida is sick. This epidemic is stealing my children, and I don't know what to do." She began to shake, giving in to great waves of emotion that consumed her. "I think strong winds are spreading the disease, and I can't do anything to stop them."

"You did for me," I whispered.

Grief filled me when I looked at my mother's sorrow, and I was determined to ease her pain in any way I could.

"The doctor did a tracheostomy on Ida," she explained, a little calmer but still struggling. "Just like the one you had, but Ida is not as strong as you, and I'm not sure she will survive. I fear the younger children will also become sick."

Guilt flooded me. What did I do to give Ida my disease? We did not share the same bedroom and rarely played together. During my free time, I was always at Charlie's. We had some of the same chores, but my jobs were primarily outside while hers involved helping my mother with the household work. Ida and I didn't even get along well because she liked to do girl things and I had no interest in her activities. I wanted to believe it was not my fault, but I had doubts.

As the days went by, I regained some of my strength and my voice slowly returned. Both of my parents came to comfort me and tend to my needs, but the visits were short. The rest of my siblings stayed away. I had no idea what was going on with the farm or my family.

"Henry." It was my father coming to check on me. "How are you doing today?"

"All right," I responded, but I sensed something was wrong. Fear bubbled up inside me; not the fear of danger, but the fear of not knowing what the danger was.

"Ida is gone," my father simply stated.

"What?" I shouted, ignoring the searing pain in my throat.

"The tracheostomy tube caused an infection and Ida was too weak to fight it. You were strong enough to survive, but Ida was not." Pain brewed in my father's sad blue eyes, but outwardly he remained calm.

"There will be no funeral," he continued. "We'll take her body to the graveyard next to our church. If you feel strong enough, you can ride along to say goodbye to your sister."

A numbing sense of sorrow descended on me, my body shaking as I fought for control over my emotions. Why did my family keep me so isolated? A dark feeling invaded my thoughts, and I wondered if my family blamed me for Ida's death. I was the first one to get sick, after all. I was the one who became feverish. I was the one who brought the strong winds into the house, and I was the one who survived the doctor's treatment only to spread the disease to my sister.

The following day, our entire family formed a procession to the Lutheran Cemetery. It was a sad sight to see my older brother and sisters walking alongside the wagon with the rest of us sitting next to the simple wooden coffin that was Ida's final resting place. Mother held Baby Augie in the front, and Father spoke only to the horses, urging them to pull harder. There was no funeral service, no one came to the internment. Families who knew of our situation were too frightened to attend, not knowing how long the epidemic would last, or who would be the next victim. Some families, already devastated by the disease, simply could not bear the grief.

It was the summer of 1879, and my family would have to go through this scene four more times before autumn set in: Ida, age eleven; Emilie, age eight; Helene, age six; Marie, age four; Emma, age three.

WINTER 1880–1881

Midwestern winters are famous for their extreme snow and cold. However, the winter of 1880–1881 was far beyond anything our family had ever faced. The blizzards started in October with relentless winds and eight-foot snowfalls. They would be followed by a few days of brilliant sunshine only to have the violent storms return and seep through every single crevice of our house.

It had been more than a year since my five sisters succumbed to the diphtheria epidemic, and two of my older sisters no longer lived with us, having been married the previous summer. The family remaining in our house consisted of my father and mother; my older brother, Herman; my older sister, Mathilda; my baby brother, Augie; and myself.

The unspeakable loss of five siblings destroyed my family. We all worked hard to go on with our lives, but silence was the language of our communications, and we each isolated ourselves under cloaks of sorrow. I could not look at my mother without experiencing grief. I would see images of my sisters in her every feature; her eyes, a thousand shades of blue, reminded me of Ida; her hair, a blonde mess, loosely piled on top of her head with curly bangs, the same as Emilie's; her creamy, pale skin, now a honeyed brown from hours in the sun, glowed like Emma's; hand gestures instead of words, like Helene; and the temperament of Marie.

I knew I should help with the housework, filling in for my lost sisters, but all I wanted to do was escape. The house held emptiness for me, and when inside, I felt powerless and stuck in my suffering. I yelled at my sisters, had no patience with my baby brother, and fought with my older brother, but worst of all, I could not bring myself near my inconsolable mother.

When outside of the house, I transformed into a different person who could not work hard enough, fast enough, or complete enough jobs. I gave up on childhood playtime and refused to go over to Charlie's house, even though my father said I had finished my chores and he didn't need more help. I still found things to do—milk the cows, clean the chicken coop, stack the hay, anything to keep busy. I kept going, going, going. I had to prove I was a good son who made his parents proud, not the son who brought disaster to his family.

My father and I, along with Herman, worked the farm, tending to the livestock, and planting and harvesting our crops. We were starting to use more mechanical equipment but still relied on horses, oxen, and our own manpower to operate the machines and get our produce to market. Exhaustion set in by the end of the day, but I was not finished. Following dinner, I would go to the barn to sharpen tools, clean the stalls, prepare for the following day's work, or do anything I thought would be helpful. Total exhaustion was the only thing allowing me to sleep at night.

My mother was melancholy and spent her time taking care of Baby Augie, who was now two years old. My older sister, Mathilda, was responsible for the house and did the cooking and cleaning, but only what was necessary to sustain us. We had food on the table and some clean clothes, but as the winter wore on, our meals became sparse and consisted of bread and potatoes. I would bring in wheat grain every morning from the barn and Mathilda would grind it into flour to make bread. We worried if the storms continued, our dwindling supply of food would not be enough to sustain us.

In January we had a short break in the weather, so Father and I went to town to buy supplies. Everybody talked about how hard the winter had been and what we needed to do to survive. Already, train service was unreliable, and we could not ship any crops, nor could we get supplies like fuel and groceries. Many times, the snow drifted over the train tracks, and shoveling it only created bigger drifts as the wind blew more snow into the trenches.

"How about some kerosene?" my father asked Mr. Toll, the general store owner.

"I'd love to sell you some," said Mr. Toll, "but the last of it went out this morning, and I don't know when the train will be able to get through to bring us more."

"How are we going to see anything?" my father asked.

"Same way as Abe Lincoln. Study by candlelight!" Mr. Toll replied.

"Well then, I'll just take some groceries so we can make a pot of hot beer soup to keep us warm. Bread and potatoes are getting tiresome as a dinner."

Mr. Toll gave us a perplexed look. "Don't you know we are out of sugar? You're going to have to improvise with whatever ingredients you have. Do you still have that great recipe for lager your father taught you?"

"Of course," my father replied. "I will never be without it!"

Once outside, we navigated around the immense snow piles and climbed into our wagon. Very few people were on the roads, most everyone snowed in and not able to get to town. Store fronts were impossible to see, and we could only enter through a narrow path shoveled by the owner. The road between our farm and the town was almost impassable. Old Buck struggled, his hooves slipping on the uneven ice patches and deep drifts. We looked for wood, downed trees, anything that would burn, but the snow was too deep. Everything was buried.

"We may have to cut down some trees on our property to make it through the winter," my father said.

"I promise to help you when we get home," I replied, without much enthusiasm. I was hoping we would not have to cut down my favorite tree near my mother's garden. I would be sad remembering how we all used to play there in the summer when we were a complete family.

On the way home, I became nervous thinking about being confined in our house all winter with few supplies and limited food. I tried to think of something to talk about to get my mind off the storm and turn to more pleasant thoughts.

"Dad," I began. "You never talk much about your family and how we got the farm. I know we are one of the bigger farms in the area, but did you inherit it from your parents? What ever happened to your other brothers or sisters?"

My father gave me a quizzical look. "You never seemed much interested in my family, so I never talked about it. Besides, my family was mostly girls, and they all went off and got married. I was left with the farm."

"Yeah, but . . ." I pushed, "I thought you had a brother too. Why didn't he get the farm, or at least share it with you?"

"Are you sure you want to know this whole story? It's not something I like to think about."

I didn't know what to say. I was trying to lift his spirits and take our minds off our problems, but now it seemed as if I brought up more bad memories. "I do want to know." Nothing a brother could do would be as bad as what I had already done to our family.

"I suppose, since you asked." He cleared his throat, his forehead wrinkled. "There is a reason I never talk much about my family. My brother, Charles, was born a deaf-mute, which means he couldn't hear, so he never learned to talk. People thought he was just dumb, but I used to play with him when we were kids. As we got older, I assumed the responsibilities of the farm, but Charles could not. My parents, while I believed they loved him, did not know what to do with him, and Charles stayed as far away from the family as he could. He wandered around by himself until one day he got into an accident. He was walking on the train tracks and couldn't hear the approaching train in time to jump out of the way. His right leg was cut off."

I stared at my father in disbelief. "Did he survive?"

"He lived, but my parents changed after that incident. They no longer wanted Charles around, and he became an unwanted person who was always in the way. My father especially couldn't deal with a son who could not follow in his footsteps, and he finally decided to put him in a place where he would get more care."

My father paused, taking in a long breath.

"A few years later, Charles died while still living in the institution. My parents went to collect his earthly goods but left his remains to be buried in the potter's field, a pauper's grave. An obituary in the *Brandon Times* had critical remarks about my parents that I will never forget."

"What did it say?" I asked.

He sighed. "'And may God have mercy on their poor, stingy souls.' It was a hurtful statement, and Charles was never talked about again."

I wanted to speak, say something comforting, but my father just looked at Buck's feet trudging through the frozen snow.

"In truth," my father continued, "my parents were not

stingy and had paid for his care. They were just incapable of
dealing with a son who was not normal. At home, I tried to
make everything return to normal, but it never did."

My father paused, lost in his memories before he went on.
"This all happened long before I met your mother and started
having children of my own. I will always remember, though,
what it feels like to be helpless in dealing with tragedy."

"I know what it feels like," I replied with disdain. I was
thinking of the tragedy I had brought to my family. I was
the one who had allowed the strangling angel to enter our
home.

Silence followed, but I was sure my father could read
my thoughts, and he knew I was no longer thinking about
Charles but of my sisters. "Sometimes, Henry," he said, "you
do everything you can, but nothing works out right. Charles
couldn't help that he was a deaf mute, but he didn't punish
himself the way you do."

"I guess you're right, but I can't help it," I said. "I just can't
hide behind a happy face."

"I think we need to find wood and get home to the others,"
my father said. He, too, wanted to think of happier moments.
"In spite of this cold weather and lack of supplies, we'll figure
out something to do tonight to get us through this long winter.
C'mon, Buck!"

Back at home, my father decided to make beer soup, even
though we didn't have all the ingredients. We got eggs from
our hen house and found some brick cheese we had been given
by Chester Hazen. In our barn, we stored the lager and were
eager to tap into the keg. We looked forward to the treat, and
even my mother showed a hint of enjoyment. We tried so hard
to be happy.

I stoked the fire in the hearth, being careful to conserve our use of wood. We lit candles instead of kerosene lamps, creating a warm glow in the house. When the soup was finished, we devoured it, which somehow made the bread and potatoes taste special.

After dinner, we got out straws of wheat and tried to play pick-up sticks. The only problem was the wheat was so dry it kept breaking, and all we did was make a mess and waste our precious supply of food. We moved on to tiddlywinks, which tested our skills at snapping wooden chips into a jar. Herman was the winner, but I think my father let him win. We all enjoyed the games, and I started to remember we could have fun as a family.

I glanced at the photograph above the hearth and remembered the family posing for the camera. We hired a real photographer because my parents wanted the entire family in the picture. I complained because I didn't like standing still that long and I especially didn't like standing between my sisters. I scowled and fidgeted the whole time, making my parents mad. But now I saw that picture differently. There we all were in front of our house, a complete family. It made me sad to see our family cut in half and I was to blame. Five of my sisters were gone because I ruined everything with my carelessness. Nothing would ever be the same. The scowling boy in the photograph needed to be punished.

In February, we got the worst snowstorm ever in an already record-breaking winter. It started one afternoon when the clouds began to gather in dark, billowing masses, causing night to set in early. Soon the snow started to fall, slowly at first, but it quickly turned into a horizontal blur as the winds picked up. I lay in bed that night, unable to sleep, and listened to the howling wind as the cold, frigid air seeped through our walls and windows. My down blanket was not enough to keep me warm, so I climbed into bed with my brother, hoping for more warmth from his body heat, but I remained cold and shivering.

The winds and snow howled all night, and I awoke the next morning to a continuation of the storm. Slowly opening my eyes, I saw a puff of a smokey cloud billow out of my mouth. I gasped for air, but my throat constricted as the cold entered. The air was painful. A thick layer of ice had formed on the inside pane of the window, and frost and snow rested on the windowsill below.

By the third day, the snow outside reached my windowsill on the second story of our house, burying the lower half of the house and trapping everyone inside. Scraping the ice off the window and looking outside, I saw an unending blanket of white looking back at me, with no definition of fields, garden, road, fence, log piles, or haystacks. Only the top of our barn and boughs of trees were exposed, but even they were covered with thick, fluffy white snow pillows. It was a fairy tale world, beautiful in any other situation, if only the snow would stop.

Running downstairs in a panic, I shouted that we were going to be buried alive inside our house if the snow didn't stop. Huddled in front of the fireplace, my parents, along with my two married sisters and their husbands, sat in close contact trying to keep each other warm. My sister Louisa was crying, saying she couldn't take it any longer. They had arrived the night before to stay with us because they had no wood for heat or food to eat at their house. My other sister, Ann, arrived earlier in the day, asking if she and her husband could stay since they could not live in their small, cold house. They brought some kerosene but had no food or wood. My parents were happy to have everybody home, but they didn't know how we were all going to survive on what meager supplies we had.

The first floor of our house was completely dark, every

window blocked by the snow. The front door only opened slightly where Ann's husband had dug an opening, but it soon filled with snow and trapped us inside. My mother lit some candles, and once the fire in the hearth was burning brighter, we sat down to talk about what we needed to do to survive.

Gradually, the room became warmer. My father took charge. "We need to work together if we are going to survive this storm," he said. "First of all, we need to bring everything we can from the second floor into the kitchen area. That includes all clothes, blankets, pillows, and any bedding. We are not going to try to heat the upstairs but rather live in the downstairs and keep each other warm. Being buried in the snow is actually a good thing because it keeps the wind out of the house and any heat we have will stay on the inside."

I thought my father was the smartest person around, because he was going to find a way to get us through this horrible storm.

"We also need to find a way to get to our barn," he continued. "The livestock need to be fed, the cows still need to be milked, and the chickens need food and warmth. We need to do this right away."

We all stared at each other in silence until my father said, "We need to tunnel our way to the barn and the chicken coop. Oh, also the outhouse!"

Building an underground tunnel system was going to be a challenge and take planning and hard work. We drew a map of the paths we needed and divided them into segments. My father assigned each family member a specific task, but I volunteered to start the tunnel to the outhouse since I needed to get there right away.

Everybody bundled up in their warmest clothes and grabbed whatever utensils or tools they could find to battle the forces of nature raging outside. I used a frying pan for a shovel and went upstairs to climb out of the second story window and into the snow. The rest of my family followed until we were all outside, braving the elements. Without proper equipment, it was slow going, but we gradually started to make progress.

The snow continued all day, and we had to be careful of the wind direction so the snow we removed didn't simply create bigger drifts and make our job harder. My two brothers-in-law made their way to the barn so they could get some of our supplies and take care of the livestock. They started at the top, even with the roofline, and dug a well eight feet down through the snow so we could open the barn door. My father and Herman started at the house and tunneled their way toward the barn with my father shoveling snow while my brother hauled it away in a bucket. He took the bucket into the house so the snow could melt. I started at the outhouse and worked my way toward the main tunnel. My sisters dug another well to get into the chicken coop. Luckily, we had surrounded the coop in the fall with bales of hay for insulation, so the chickens were safe and could survive the cold weather.

We worked like this all day until we finally had enough tunnels to get where we needed to go to care for our animals. My mother and sisters made dinner, bread, and potatoes again, but with a few eggs thrown in to make it extra delicious. We were all exhausted, so we lay down on the floor, fighting to see who could get closest to the fire, and settled in for the night. Our house had not been this full of people for a long time, and it was comforting to know we were all together. I watched my mother taking care to make sure everyone had enough blankets; she almost seemed happy to oversee something.

On the fifth day of the never-ending storm, I followed my father into the barn to help with the livestock. The cows were jittery, and old Buck looked sad and weary. I watched my father work on the horse's harness, trying to clean the bit and get the joints to move smoothly. My mind started to wander back to the horrible summer of '79, and I couldn't understand how he was able to go on with life after the death of five daughters. My father was obviously heartbroken, but the tragedy did not affect his work the way it did my mother's, or the rest of our family's. He seemed to be the same person he always had been. He stared at me.

"Why do you work so hard?" he asked.

He was looking at my red, raw hands as I untangled the harnesses. I didn't know why he was concerned because the pain didn't bother me, and the excessive work was just part of my life.

"They don't really hurt much. I've been cold for so long I don't even notice it anymore."

"No, I don't mean your hands. I mean, why do you push yourself to do more work than anyone else in the family?"

"I don't know," I responded. "I just want to help."

"You can't make things better by working yourself to the bone. What if you get sick?"

"I won't get sick," I snapped, glaring at him.

A silence grew between us until finally I spoke. "I can take care of myself," I said. "I want to work hard so everyone will be happy with me."

He put a hand on my shoulder. "Henry, no matter what you do, the family will always love you. Just remember, though, there will always be some people who disagree with you. You can't take it upon yourself to please everyone."

My father continued working on the harnesses, and I figured our talk was over. Since I wanted to learn how to harness the horses to the buggy, I thought this was a good time to ask.

"Can you teach me how to put these harnesses on the horses?" I asked.

"Okay," my father began. "It's time you learn. Never approach a horse from the back. Even an old horse like Buck will get startled if you come at him from his blind side. Always let him see you approach, or he might kick you."

I watched my father work the bit into Buck's mouth as he explained what to do. When my father finished, he turned to me with a smile. "If you're interested, I have another story I think you're finally old enough to understand. It's about my time in the army. For many years, I was unable to talk about it, but you should listen to this story and tell me what you think."

"I didn't know you were in the war that was fought in the South," I said. "Did you fight the rebels?"

"Not exactly," my father replied. "At twenty-nine years old, I was sent to Camp Randall in Madison to train to be a soldier. Initially, I didn't want to go because I already had the farm, a wife, and three children. After thinking about it, I decided that, as an immigrant, I should show my adopted country I could be a good soldier for the Union Army and contribute however I could. It was December of 1864."

I could almost see a physical transformation come over my father as he started to talk about the war. There was sorrow in his voice, and his eyes became unfocused as he stared at the bales of hay stacked at the back of the barn. He was not a person who showed a lot of emotion, but I could feel a tension surrounding him. I knew this was something important to him, as well as to me. I felt honored to be trusted with this information.

"Once in Louisiana, we settled into a tented camp with other soldiers who had been there for a while. It was March, and our company was needed to replace soldiers who were sick or dead.

Our orders were to capture the Confederate stronghold at Fort Blakeley. I hated Louisiana. It was hot, there was no clean water, men were packed into small tents, everyone seemed sick with fevers and diarrhea, and the food was awful. I was a simple farm boy from Wisconsin who didn't know anything about living in what seemed like a foreign land, and before long, I too became sick. We received orders to attack Fort Blakeley, and I tried to convince myself I could be an honorable and brave soldier. But I was too weak to get out of bed, much less march into battle. Most of my company left while I stayed behind.

"The Union soldiers eventually captured Fort Blakeley, thanks in no small part to the Negro company, which played a major role in the assault. We didn't know at the time, but the same day the troops captured Fort Blakeley, General Lee surrendered to Grant at Appomattox, and the war was officially over. Our battle was meaningless."

"Dad," I interrupted. "What is a Negro company?"

"We do not have Negros living near us, so it was a new experience for me to even meet one. A Negro is a person whose family descended from Africa, and most of those living in the South were slaves. There were others living in the North, but usually in the city, and they were free men."

"Were there any Negros in your company?"

"No. They had their own company and their own living quarters. My captain called them the 'Black-bellied Yankees.'"

"Why would anybody call them that? If someone called me that, I would punch them."

"You're probably right, Henry. Nobody should call people names, especially since the soldiers of the Forty-Eighth Regiment US Colored Troops probably won the battle of Fort Blakely for the Yankees."

I still could not believe that soldiers would call each other names and not fight together. I wanted to know more. "How did you meet the Negro Company?"

"I told you I was too sick to fight in the battle, but after it was over, I started to recover some of my strength. One day I took a walk out of our camp to try to get away from the sickness and stench, and I happened upon one of the Negro soldiers, who was also taking a break. His camp was a mile away, and we sat together and rested. At first he was shy, not wanting to talk to me, but I told him of my illness, and it seemed to make him more comfortable. He was an experienced soldier, unlike me, and told me about the battle, his movements, and how his unit had approached the fort. They suffered few losses because they had been held in reserve until the last rush. He gave me a lot more details, but I have forgotten most of them. What I will never forget is the gift he gave me."

My father smiled warmly.

"When each of us had to go back to our camps, my friend—I never did learn his name—reached into his pocket and pulled out a gold coin. I had never seen one before and didn't know its value, but he told me to take it. He found it on a rebel soldier but couldn't keep it because he would be accused of stealing if someone found it in his possession. I told him I would have the same problem, but he assured me I would not. I looked at the coin and saw it was a one-dollar gold piece from 1856 with Lady Liberty on one side, and the United States of America written on the back. He said he could not spend it, so I may as well take it. 'Maybe it will bring you luck,' he said. I thanked him and we parted ways.

"As I walked back to the camp, I felt the coin jiggle in my pocket. For some unknown reason, it gave me a feeling of strength, and I decided I would never use the coin to buy anything. I would keep it as a good luck charm."

After telling me about the coin, my father walked over to his workbench and rummaged through a drawer until he found what he was looking for. He returned and placed the gold coin in my hand. "Its luck is now transferred to you," he said. "I hope you will keep it safe."

"I can't take this from you," I said. "I don't deserve to have luck and I don't want to take it away from you. You've earned it."

My father looked tired, needing a rest. His face fell into an expression I had never seen before, a vulnerability he kept hidden. "No Henry, you have earned it. I want you to have it."

"Thank you," I said. "You have no idea what this means to me." As I wrapped my fingers around the coin, a current of joy surged through my body. "Can you tell me more about what happened after the war ended?"

My father's expression changed when I asked him to tell me more. He continued. "I stayed in the army for another few months as we marched to Mobile and then Montgomery, but I was always afraid of getting sick again and disappointing the other men in my infantry, not to mention my country. I believed the gold coin kept me safe and I always carried it with me. I was a little superstitious back then because I didn't know that disease and sanitation were linked, just like nobody knows what brings on a diphtheria epidemic. Someday someone will discover the cause, but for now, we still struggle."

Hearing this, I realized he wasn't talking about himself anymore but trying to reach out to me. He continued. "When I got home after the war, I could not talk about my experience and only wanted to get back to the farm where I felt safe. I worked hard, just like you are doing now, because I felt a responsibility to make things right after having failed so horribly in service to my country. My family was happy to have me home and didn't seem to notice my sadness or guilt; at least I hoped I was fooling them.

"Over time, everything returned to normal. Mathilda was born and life moved on. I learned many soldiers had died of dysentery, and I was one of the lucky ones who recovered. The guilt gradually went away when I finally realized the only one who thought I was a failure was me. My family just wanted me home. The hard work was necessary to run the farm but not necessary to prove I was good."

That day in the barn, with the wind howling outside and our bodies cold from the numbing winter, I started to feel a little warmth on the inside. My strong, silent father had bad memories and feelings of guilt, but he survived and so should I.

After our talk, I went back to work. My hands were still red and raw, my body was still sore and cold, and the never-ending snow was still falling, but I was thinking about the way I tended to punish myself with excessive work. Was that necessary? Did anybody blame me for the death of my sisters other than me?

The snow lasted for nine days, a record I was sure would never be broken. Our family lived in darkness most of the time, having run out of kerosene on day four, but we were all together. Our tunnels allowed us to maintain the farm, although we did lose some of the chickens and we went to bed hungry many nights. We stayed warm because of the closeness of our bodies as we huddled together in the only room of the house that was slightly heated. Every one of us had the will and determination to survive.

Once the storm subsided, a thaw came and melted the surface of the huge snowdrifts surrounding us. We feared flooding, but after three days of above-freezing temperatures, a hard freeze hit, and an impenetrable crust formed on the surface of the drifts. We thought we were in for another blizzard, and the family huddled together to make plans for the battle with Mother Nature.

The next morning, Mother and Father climbed the stairs to the second story of our house to look out the windows, expecting to see more dark clouds bringing the white monster to our house. To their surprise, the sun was a golden orb in the sky and the wind was singing a song of quiet peace. The frost on the window was twinkling in the sunlight and a winter wonderland had materialized from our frozen landscape.

Running downstairs, my mother shouted, "Everybody find your warmest clothes and blankets and come upstairs."

"Are we moving upstairs?" I asked. "It's too cold up there."

"Just come with us," my parents said. They looked happy, an unusual occurrence these days. My mother bundled up the baby, and the rest of us found whatever clothes we could throw together and climbed the stairs to do whatever it was my parents thought we should do.

"Outside," said my father. "Now!"

"What are you talking about? We'll freeze to death," we all said in unison.

My father climbed out of the window, followed by my mother, who was holding Augie. The rest of us followed, thinking our parents had lost their minds, but once outside, we saw it was beautiful. Ice covered everything and the drifts were like crystal waves flowing over the landscape. They sparkled with a rainbow of colors that beckoned us into this magical fairyland.

After everyone was outside, my father said, "Follow me." He jumped onto a drift face-first. He didn't sink but slid down the drift and out across our farmland, twisting and turning and laughing all the way until he came to a stop near the road at the edge of our property. The rest of us needed no more encouragement, and we all flew across the snow, faster than our old horse Buck could have ever run. We screamed at the sheer delight of flying across the ice.

We ended up in a big pile, crashing into one another, hysterically giggling. Living in such close quarters and being cooped up in a dark house for almost two weeks had taken its toll, but being outside in the sunshine, our spirits soared. We could not stop laughing.

The one person who was missing from this joyous bedlam was my mother. I decided to climb back up the hill to hold Augie so Mother could join the rest of the family in our fun. Getting back was exhausting, but when I reached her, she nestled Augie safely between two snow drifts and gave me a big hug. No words were spoken; they were unnecessary. I felt her warmth and energy come into my body, and the honesty of our embrace defused the bomb living inside me. I couldn't let go. We stood there for a long time, silent with our own thoughts, until Augie started to cry.

"Is it my turn to slide down?" my mother calmly looked at me, eyes brimming with tears.

"Of course," I said. "I'll watch Augie."

As my mother soared over the snow, she was no longer fragile like she had been for so long. She was strong and resilient. And so was I.

KIM

ROUND TWO

FEBRUARY 15, 2009

I just feel cursed. Will our family always be split apart by death? Death. This is all I can think about. Death is quiet. Death is peaceful. Death is total. Death stops everything. This is what I want. My death will not be physically painful; no cutting, no gasping for a last breath, only a slow weakening of my body, followed by a slow morphine drip until I fade away. It sounds inviting.

I am not afraid, but I do have questions. Where will I go? Will I be a ghost? Will I watch my family from another place? Will I be reunited with Billy? Will I be able to answer the age-old question, *Is there a God?* Or, *Should I have been more religious during my lifetime?* Death will answer these questions. I want the puzzle solved.

It has been three weeks since the first chemo session, and I suffered through it, angry and depressed the entire time. The only side effect I didn't have was nausea, but fatigue, mouth sores, and chemo brain attacked me with a vengeance. My brain took a vacation from my body, and I had trouble concentrating and focusing on anything. I reverted to my eighteen-year-old self and became a total scatterbrain, not able to remember details, common words, names, or events. These side effects lessened as time went on, but the thought of five more rounds sent me into a tailspin of depression.

Mark remained patient, kind, and helpful throughout. I resented his positivity, and hated myself for resenting it. Why isn't he feeling as weak as I am? After researching my ancestor, the one who I suspect is my great grandfather, all I could think about was the trauma of disease constantly surrounding them. He came to know death and sickness at such a young age. What kind of person did it make him? Did he think this would always haunt his family?

Ready for round two, Mark and I enter this once-perceived Zen room. Instead of the calming scent of jasmine, my nose is bombarded by the harsh undertones of bleach and antiseptics. These odors trigger a memory of sitting in the chair looking at bags of drugs and seeing my arm being punctured by needles. My stomach starts to twist.

"Mark," I say. "Do you notice anything different about this room? It's so sterile. Where did the Zen go?"

"It's a hospital, shouldn't it be sterile?" Mark says as he ushers me to the reception desk. "The Zen is still present. Can't you smell the jasmine?"

"I don't smell it at all." I stop and look at the polished surfaces, fake plants, and industrial-style chairs. "This place makes me think of a latex glove factory. It smells like rubber, and everyone is wearing white suits and masks."

"The chemo altered your senses. You will just have to live with it for a while because nothing is different," he says, his patience running thin.

"Nothing except my whole world." My face flushes and I become indignant. "I don't know what to expect from these treatments. Am I going to feel like shit again? I'm tired of being cold all the way into my core."

Drawing in a breath, trying to calm the rising storm, Mark

says. "When the chemo starts, they'll cover you with warm blankets and you'll be fine. Don't worry."

"Fine."

"Fine." Mark places his hand on my back to get me to move faster.

Before round two begins, we meet with Dr. Belmont. He walks into his office appearing cheerful and confident in his buttoned-up manner. Expecting him to deliver his usual soundbites before he sends me to "the chair," I feel a little defiant until I notice tattoos peeking out from his sleeve. I look to his face and see pierced ears, as well as space on the right side of his nose for a ring. I need to rethink my initial impression. Is it possible he is a biker disguised as a doctor?

"How were the last three weeks?" asks Dr. Belmont.

"Fine," I say as I try to make sense of his tattoo markings. "The first week was a little rough but the last half was all right."

"Good," he responds.

"What are you talking about?" Mark chimes in. "There was nothing fine about it." He turns and targets his anger at the doctor. "The side effects made her miserable. Only the last week was fine, nothing else."

"That's normal," says Dr. Belmont.

"Nothing is normal about this." I suddenly find my voice as my temples throb and pain wraps itself around my head. "I prepared both physically and mentally for this treatment, but you never told me about the fatigue. I never anticipated the total fog taking over my body and making everyday living impossible. Days without sleep made me crazy and I felt helpless."

I am silent for a moment, but since nobody else is talking I continue with my rant. "I thought I would at least be able to watch TV, read a book, carry on a conversation, or somehow relate to my family but instead I could only sit motionless, feeling miserable and constantly cold. Why didn't you tell me what to expect?"

Dr. Belmont keeps his composure. "Every patient is different," he says, "and not all side effects are the same. We don't know ahead of the treatment what your reaction will be, but I can tell your body handled the treatment well. Your blood work is looking better already."

I stare at him. "I thought I was suffering through each day and you're telling me I did well?"

"It's possible the reason you were so miserable was because the drugs killed a lot of the cancer cells, causing you discomfort. They are supposed to do that."

"Will each session be the same?"

"We have to wait and see," says the doctor. He's back to his soundbites.

"Fine," I say, looking at my tightly folded hands with their swollen joints and age spots. I pause for a moment before asking, "By the way, do you own a Harley?"

"What the . . ." Mark looks at me in disbelief at how random my thoughts are. He stands, gently grabbing my arm so he can get me out of there.

Dr. Belmont turns and smiles as he leaves. "Yes, I do."

"It's nice to see a crack in the façade," I say as I pull away from Mark and march toward the big chemo chair. I take my place in front of the window and the nurse brings over a warm blanket as she hooks me up to the IV. Outside, the weather matches my mood: cold, dark, and ominous. Nobody is riding bikes or walking in the park. The dark clouds along the horizon swell like waves and threaten a winter storm. During the first round of chemo the lake was joyful, a brilliant turquoise absorbing all the sunshine from above, but today it is a moody, turbulent swirl of water with pillars of steam rising like ghostly figures.

Mark and I settle in. He looks at me and says, "I like it when you challenge the doctor. The meek, compliant Kim doesn't suit you."

"I want Dr. Belmont to understand my inner misery. He needs to treat me as an individual, not an illness. I think I got him at the end when I asked him about a Harley."

"I know what you mean. He did show a glimmer of humanity today," Mark says, "but he is so obsessed with himself that he can't connect to you as a person."

"You're right," I reply, glancing at the drips coming out of the IV. "Sorry about my attitude. He's just so mechanical in speaking to me I want to shake him up."

"I get the point." Mark relaxes into his chair and reaches into his pocket to get the Rubik's Cube he always carries.

"Haven't you solved that puzzle yet?" I ask. "I thought your mathematical mind would have every square lined up by now."

"This is more than math," Mark responds, staring intently at the puzzle. "When I bought this, it was perfect, each face one solid color. I made a few moves and now I can't get it back together. I can't figure it out. I'm a math nerd. I was never good at solid geometry."

"Give it time. You'll find a way."

Mark gets lost in his jumbled, pattern-less mess of colors. Closing my eyes, I am transported to another place, a place where I am not pitied or patronized. Whenever I think of death, I view it as a painful truth, a dark and treacherous road everyone must travel before reaching a clearing. It may be that death is not my final destination. What if there is more? Maybe death is the middle of my story, and I am on a path to a place beyond. Is there a place beyond?

Sometimes when I'm walking on that path I see Billy, distant but visible. His image merges with my great grandfather as both suffered with an illness they didn't understand. The difference was that Billy's illness was hidden. Is this road my future?

Mark and I have not discussed my feelings about dying beyond our initial conversation. I am conflicted but have not changed my mind. Putting away the Rubik's Cube, Mark opens his email and begins to work. He lives in a world of well-defined rules and predictable outcomes while uncertainty dominates mine. I hate uncertainty.

The hazmat nurse interrupts my musing and says, "Time for the red drug. I'll slow the drips so you don't get irritation in your nose."

Practicing my pleasant conversational skills, I ask, "How long did it take you to learn the names of all these drugs? I've been told their names several times but the only one I remember is prednisone."

"I'm licensed as an oncology nurse," she answers. "It took about a year before I became certified, and it took a lot of memorizations and a good refresher course in Latin!"

"I once took a course where I had to use Latin to memorize the botanical names of trees," I proudly announce. "I think memorizing those names added wrinkles to my brain."

"I certainly added wrinkles to my brain by learning all those drug names," the nurse says as she walks away.

"What was that all about?" Mark asks. "She's not interested in your trees or your Latin. The drugs are getting to you."

"What do you know?" I say with a haughty attitude. "I just didn't want to talk about cancer." I look away and mutter, "I think she does care about my trees."

Halfway through the treatment, Mark takes a break to get something to eat. To my surprise and delight, Julie stops in for a visit. She enters like a breath of fresh air, and I feel better just knowing she is there. People have told us we look alike, but I never saw the similarity until recently. She is a little shorter than I am, but both of us have our mother's slim build; delicate, symmetrical features; and a fair complexion. The golden hair of our youth is now a darker ash blonde, periodically highlighted by chemicals of a non-medical nature. Our ocean-blue eyes, round and full, are our most striking feature; they sparkle with light as we smile, and we smile often, or at least I use to.

"How are you doing?" Julie asks.

"I'm okay," I say. "It's hard to say 'good' when you're sitting in a chemo chair."

"Remember, when Mom was sick, they didn't even have chemotherapy back then."

"And she suffered greatly. I don't want to suffer the way she did."

"You won't," Julie encourages. "They have better drugs today."

"Right, and I plan to use them."

Julie and I became close once we got past the childhood years of "That's mine," or "You're touching me." Now we enjoy our time together and can talk forever about a wide assortment of topics both of our husbands find tedious. When our mother died, Julie was the only person in the room who knew my feelings and now I need her. She is the one who understands me.

"Thank you for the book of our family's history," I say and smile as I reach for my glass of ginger ale. "I loved all the pictures. Some people I remembered but others I didn't know."

"I've done a lot of research going to cemeteries, exploring Ancestry.com, and looking at old records."

"How far back were you able to go?" I ask. "I didn't recognize anybody from those old pictures."

"The earliest record I found was from 1847. Remember how we always thought our family came to the US around the turn of the century? They were actually here a lot earlier."

"One picture caught my attention, the one you labeled 'The Gaugers.' Is that the family you told me about who lost five of their daughters in one summer to diphtheria? What happened to them?"

"The mother went on to have three more children."

"Those were obviously the days before birth control. What a woman!"

"That was not uncommon back then," Julie adds. "The son who survived the epidemic was Henry, our great-grandfather. I put a later picture of him in the book, living on a farm with his two sons, one of whom is Clarence, our grandfather."

I smile when I realize my intuition was correct. "Do you know which of the children in the earlier family picture is Henry? There's one boy who I think looks like me. He's the one looking away with a look of devilry in his eyes."

"It could be him, but it's hard to tell," Julie adds. "I know at one time Henry owned the farm because I found a record of the deed in my research."

"I have the book with me," I say, reaching into my cancer tote bag. "Show me the later picture of Henry?"

Julie pages through the book until she finds a picture of a farmer standing next to an old house, holding a pitchfork in one hand with two ragged-looking boys leaning in on him. It resembles the American Gothic painting, only fifty years early, and with a farmhouse instead of a gothic building.

"I'm pretty sure this is Henry and his twin sons."

"If Henry is our great-grandfather, then one of those boys is Clarence, our grandfather."

I take a closer look at the photo. The boy on the left has eyes of pure mischief and probably a DNA that spells fun while the other boy is the serious one. Both have unruly blond hair dominating a round face with big eyes. The photo is black and white, but I'm sure the color of their eyes is blue and the skin pale. Their faded jeans and old T-shirts are too small and sit on wiry frames which makes them seem even more skinny. Physically, they look alike, but their body language tells me their souls beat to different drums.

I page through the book looking for information about the Gauger family. There aren't any more pictures, but I find a short newspaper article in the "What's Happening" section called Twin vs. Twin. "What's this?" I ask Julie.

"This is typical small-town news. They record every event, every social gathering, every court ruling, and I cut this one out because I thought it might be connected to the Gaugers."

I skim the story with renewed interest while Julie searches for Clarence's diary in my tote bag. "This article is about two brothers, Clarence and Ernie, who sued each other. Do you know anything about this?" I ask.

Julie opens the diary and says, "It appears there is some mystery in our family surrounding certain events involving Clarence and his brother. The diary sheds some light on what happened, but you should read it yourself to get a better understand."

I open the diary to my bookmarked page and say, "I only read as far as the section where Clarence talks about how hard it was to move to Milwaukee. Mom told us he was lost until he met Grandma and started working for her father's newspaper. I always thought he was a wild and crazy guy?"

"Yes, he was." Julie smiles at the recollection. "I remember him from when we were kids. He lived in a big house and Mom was close to him, but I don't think Dad liked him."

"He also is the one who took us to a baseball game and offered us beer. We were twelve at the time."

Julie laughs. "True, his background may be mysterious, but I remember him as a fun-loving guy. I actually took a few sips of that beer and liked it!"

"I think he died shortly after the baseball incident. Maybe Mom's anger drove him to an early grave."

"I doubt that," Julie says. "You know how easygoing Mom was. If anybody drove him to an early grave, it was Dad. He was a bear to get along with. I don't know how Mom did it."

"Or how we survived living with him. It was not easy, as I recall."

We return to the scrapbook. My grandfather Clarence looked like a scrappy, disheveled kid in the photo with his father and brother. Fists clenched, eyes brooding, mouth in a tight line, he looks like a scamp. But his body language tells a different story. He is leaning into his father, as if needing physical contact or maybe security. A later picture shows an adult Clarence with his daughter, Lizzie, at a political event with balloons falling from the ceiling of a large auditorium. His posture is upright, his hands outstretched, and a burst of happiness is spread across his face. What transformed the brooding farm boy into the smiling adult? I remember him fondly from my teen years and want to believe I inherited some of his adventurous spirit and craziness. Could it be tucked away somewhere within my personality?

"Do you know if anyone in our family had cancer besides Mom? I'm wondering if cancer genes run in our family."

"I couldn't tell you. Census records and death certificates from back then don't give medical information."

"I guess it will remain a mystery."

Julie and I continue to peruse the book and look back into our past. We identify family members and compare our shared memories. It is remarkable how different those memories are, given we were in the same place at the same time, but we have different recollections of what happened.

By the time Mark gets back from his lunch break, all he hears from us is the unconcealed laughter of friends and the relaxed joy of familiarity.

"I love you," I say to Julie. "You always know how to brighten my day."

Hearing the laughter in my voice as Julie leaves, Mark looks wistful as his eyes follow her to the exit. "Looks like you had a good time with Julie."

"We talked about our ancestors and tried to decide what characteristics we inherited from each of them."

"What did you discover?" Mark's interest is piqued.

"Julie found some pictures and government records from the late 1800s. Here, take a look. This one is of the entire Gauger family."

I hand my book to Mark. "I think I am a direct descendent of a determined, hardworking family. Look at the hard line of everyone's jaw, the rigid bodies, the seriousness of their expressions."

"Are you sure that's not simply the way people posed for pictures back then?"

"Possibly," I am disheartened by Mark's inability to follow my fantasies. "I know both my great-grandfather and grandfather were independent thinkers and wanted to follow their own path. Kind of like me, developing an independent therapy practice rather than the more secure work in a hospital clinic."

Mark examines the Gauger picture more closely. "You're right about this kid. I bet it's Henry because he is not lining up like everyone else. He's different, maybe resisting authority. This is definitely your ancestor."

"Do you think I'm like that?" Mark upsets me with his condescending tone. "I follow the rules, when necessary, but I can think for myself."

"If you say so."

I feel myself slipping into the depressed version of me and I look around for the nurse to interrupt this conversation. My chemo is almost done for the day, so I need to get ready to face the cold outside, which is not that different from the chill I feel inside.

Mark breaks the silence. "Did Julie have any insights on medical conditions in the family?"

"Not really."

Mark, still trying to make conversation, asks, "Did she find any scandals in your family history that you're hiding?"

"No, nothing like that." I pause a long time, hesitant to say more. I don't want to tell Mark about my grandfather's diary because I have not read it in its entirety. It may contain emotional stories or tragedies I do not want to talk about. I want to end this conversation.

"I'm almost done with the drips. Can we go straight home?" I ask.

Mark looks out the window at the waves lapping the shoreline, beautiful but cold and icy. "I guess so. Nothing else is going on."

Plenty is going on. In my head, at least. When I go home I just want to make a project of learning more about the family. In between the gaps, I can always fill in more of the story with what I imagine life was like.

THE GAUGERS

THE TWINS

HENRY
1912

"Good morning, Henry," said Dr. Fischer. "How's my favorite patient?"

I loved the friendly warmth of our longtime family doctor. I knew him since childhood when he accompanied his father, the senior Dr. Fischer, on house visits into the rural areas. Luckily, he didn't come with his dad during the diphtheria epidemic because we later learned how dangerous that would have been. I was one of the lucky few to survive the disaster.

"I'm okay for now," I responded. "But I worry the surgery to remove the melanoma on my back was not completely successful. I tire easily and don't have my usual level of energy."

"Let's take a look," said the doctor.

I sat on the examining table and took off my shirt. "I hope the surgery got everything because I don't think I can afford another medical procedure," I said as I tried to read Dr. Fischer's facial expression. A look of concern crossed his face as he examined the surgical area. His brows tightened and his pursed lips gave me the impression of someone ready to deliver bad news.

"How does it look?" I asked.

"There is some redness around the surgical area, but it's too early to tell. It's only been two weeks since you had the surgery."

"I know, but I worry about it coming back and being malignant. If it is fatal, what would happen to my twins?"

"Recurrence is always a possibility," Dr. Fischer explained. "You are fair-skinned with blond hair and blue eyes. You work outside so your skin is constantly exposed to the elements which can be risk factors."

"What should I do?"

"For now, you just have to wait and see if you heal properly. The boys are adults and should be able to help you on the farm. That should take away some of the fatigue. What do they say about your condition?"

I hesitated to respond, knowing this was an issue I had been avoiding. "I haven't told them about it yet. Ernie is away at school, and Clarence and I have difficulty talking with each other."

"I would suggest you tell your boys what is going on with you. I'm sure they'd want to know."

On my way home, I couldn't shake the dark cloud hanging over me. The surgery removed not only the visible signs of the disease but also the tissues beneath and around it. It left a huge hole in my back that was visible when I took off my shirt. If the melanoma returned, I would have to tell Clarence and Ernie since it could be fatal. It was at times like this that I missed Helen, the boys' mother, the most. She would have known what to do.

I thought back to my childhood. I was nine when I suffered from diphtheria and Helen was a year younger. She was the sister of my best friend, Charlie, and their sibling, Emma, was one of the first children in the area to die from the epidemic. I survived, and neither Charlie nor Helen ever got sick. They were lucky. We all lived with the sadness of loss.

One day Helen asked, "Hey, can I play with you guys up in

the hay loft?" I said sure, but Charlie had a different point of view.

"No!" Charlie shouted at her as he looked at me with determination. "We have our territory, and no girls—or, for that matter, no other kids—can enter. It's private property."

"C'mon, Charlie, she's not so bad," I pleaded. "She's strong enough to lift a bale of hay and she could help us build our fort. If you don't want her inside the fort, we can make her a bad guy to keep her out. It might even be fun to chase her around."

"Okay," Charlie said, turning to look at our partially completed fort. "But only if she doesn't try to boss us around."

"She won't," I said. "I learned a lot last year, and sometimes girls are fun, maybe even useful."

Now, years later, I wondered if Helen realized what she set in motion when she asked if she could help us build our fort. Before that, Charlie and I treated her badly, excluding her from our activities, but after the diphtheria epidemic, everything changed. I was sullen and moody, and even though I still played with Charlie, there was something missing from the easygoing fun we'd once had.

Playing side-by-side with Helen, I noticed she was fun and had different ideas on how to build the fort. She even helped us set it up to keep the other kids away. Despite Charlie's insisting girls were not allowed, we included Helen in our play.

Gradually, Helen and I became constant companions. One harvest season, at the end of the day, she brought me some gooseberries and nuts along with a cold drink. After that, I saw a different girl: not my playmate, but someone I wanted to share my thoughts with. We spent time together sitting in my mother's garden between the rows of beets, potatoes, carrots, onions, and flowers.

One day, I watched Helen in the garden picking lettuce and thought to myself, *She's the one.*

"What do you want to do after high school is over?" I asked her.

I was sixteen at the time. Helen was fifteen.

"I don't know," she said. "I like living on the farm and don't think I would enjoy city life. At times living here is difficult, but despite the callouses on my hands, I want the open space and fresh air. I would feel cramped living in an apartment in the city."

"I feel the same way," I said.

I was so enamored with Helen I couldn't help blurting out, "Do you ever think we could live together on our own farm? I mean together, always?"

Though I stumbled over my words, nervously shifting my weight back and forth, Helen seemed to get my meaning. She didn't answer right away but smiled at me with the prettiest look I had ever seen. Her gentle features, the mischievous grin, and the glow in her eyes all made me feel alive. I loved her, and it was the happiest day of my life.

I married Helen in a simple ceremony at the Lutheran church next to the cemetery where five of my sisters lay in our family plot. The day was lovely; a sunlit blue glow filled the air and surrounded Helen with a magical radiance. Crocuses and daffodils bloomed in bursts of color near the entryway to the church and the fragrant scent of apple blossoms heightened my love.

Once married, we built a house in the far corner of my family's property and I began to plow, disk, drag, and cultivate the crops. I knew every inch of the land and found the best grazing for our cows, the best soil for our crops, and the best way to get those products to market. When Helen got pregnant, we were overjoyed.

"I'm having trouble sleeping," she said one morning after a restless night. "I've gotten so big I feel like a cow. In fact, not even the cows are as big as I am."

"Let's go see Dr. Fischer to make sure everything is all right," I said. "I can take some supplies into town, and you can ride in the wagon with me."

"You're going to have to help me into the wagon because I can't get my belly off the ground."

"You are not that big," I said. "You're just a little over-whelmed by the changes to your body."

"Changes, you say! You try going through a total transform-ation where you can't bend, walk, sit, or, most distressingly, sleep. This baby inside me is having a good time playing with my innards."

At least Helen had not lost her sense of humor. I laughed at how she described herself because all I saw was the beautiful mother of my future child. It may be twins, Dr. Fischer said as her belly expanded. We were thrilled. We discussed what needed to be done and how we were going to manage the next month.

When it came time for the delivery, Helen went into distress and the labor went on too long. The midwife did what she could to deliver the babies, and both boys were born healthy, but at a severe cost. There was nothing they could do to save my beloved Helen. The strain of delivering two boys and the loss of blood was too much; she passed away, leaving me with my two sons and more grief than I knew how to bear.

My entire family, as well as Helen's, attended the funeral at our local church. Charlie was there with his wife and infant son, and the look on his face showed the misery he felt. The service was brief, followed by the burial in our family plot. I spoke to no one, only listened to the cold howl of the wind, knowing my days in the sun were now over.

We all returned to my family's home where two of my sisters, Louisa and Mathilda, were taking care of my twins, Clarence and Ernie. I could not hold them. I was the one who needed comforting; they didn't know their mother was gone. My sisters gave them warmth and love. I remained alone with my sorrow and frozen tears.

"Come and have some food," I heard my mother say.

"I'm not hungry."

In the past, my mother and I could always understand each other without verbal communication. Looking at her now, I saw tension on her face, a rigid posture and clasped hands squeezed tightly together. I knew she had something to say.

"We need to talk about the twins," she started. "They must not feel your sadness. I think they should stay with us for a while until you're feeling better."

I knew she was right. "I don't know how to take care of babies, and I miss Helen so much I don't want to try."

"All of that will change in time," my mother continued. "I also think you should come home for a while and not be alone in your house. You need to have family around."

"Let me think about it," I said. "Can Louisa and Mathilda care for the twins?"

"Of course they can, and they will be happy to do it. We are family."

My mother gently touched my arm, gave me a brief smile, and went off to attend to other family members.

I spent most of the following month's longing for what no longer existed. I temporarily moved into my parents' house with my boys, but I felt empty inside. Gradually, I realized I needed to go on with my life and become the father Helen would be proud of.

One night, looking at Clarence and Ernie in their makeshift cribs, I spoke to them for the first time. "You are both beautiful, just like your mother. She would be so proud."

The next day, I held Clarence for the first time since Helen had died, and my world restarted as he looked at me and smiled. I felt a tingling sensation throughout my body and my hands touching his delicate skin linked us together as family. Something opened in my heart and a new love began to grow, a love I never knew I had.

My twins resembled the Gauger family, with their ocean-blue eyes and platinum fuzz on their heads. I knew the fuzz would turn into white gold as they grew. Clarence was a little more colicky than Ernie and never slept through the night, but both boys seemed happy. They cried and pooped and threw up, but that did not take away from the newfound happiness they brought me.

Twenty years later, Ernie was in school, and Clarence was still a little colicky. I should have known despite being twins, they were very different people.

"Clarence," I yelled. "Are you around? You're supposed to milk the cows."

No answer.

I went out to the barn. "Clarence, where are you?"

No answer.

One of the farm hands came in and said, "Clarence left about an hour ago. Said he'd be back later."

"Did he milk the cows?" I asked.

"I don't think so. He just said he was meeting some friends."

This was so typical of Clarence. He was immature and

unready for responsibility. All he thought about was fun. He deliberately opposed rules and we got into constant power struggles, often ending in arguments.

I decided to milk the cows by myself and have dinner alone. "What if I really am sick and dying?" I said to no one. "Will Clarence and Ernie be capable of running the farm together?" I had no idea. Ernie had a strong work ethic, but Clarence only wanted to play. I was also concerned about the fact that Clarence was in love. He didn't seem able to focus on anything but his girlfriend, Molly, and had no room in his heart for farming.

I fell asleep trying to think of a way to get both of my sons together on a plan for the farm. We needed to modernize and make the work less strenuous and more efficient. I just wasn't sure if the boys could work together. Had Clarence ever worked at anything? I fell asleep without any answers.

The next morning, after milking the cows, I walked into the house expecting a full breakfast waiting for me. Making breakfast was Clarence's responsibility.

"Clarence!" I yelled. "Where's my breakfast?"

"Ahh." I heard a muffled sound coming from Clarence's room.

"I said, I want breakfast." I walked into Clarence's room and could smell the stale air of a night spent in the local tavern. Clarence was lying on top of his bed, fully clothed and snoring, his long blond hair strung across his face, covering his eyes.

"Clarence!" I shouted. "Where is my breakfast and why are you still in bed? There is work to do, and it's not going to get done if you don't get up this very minute."

Clarence groaned. "Go away. I'll do it in a minute. I'm begging you, leave me alone."

His speech was slow and fuzzy, and I could hear his lips

smacking as he tried to find saliva in his mouth. He looked parched and dehydrated. I walked over to his bed and shook him forcefully until he turned and looked at me. His eyes were sunken and threaded with red veins. I gave him another push and he fell out of bed.

"What are you doing? Can't you see I'm sick and can't work today? I need you to leave me alone." Clarence struggled to his feet, moaning under his breath. "I have better things to do than make your breakfast. You just don't get it."

He staggered out of the room and went to the outhouse in the backyard. I watched as he attempted to keep his balance while he stumbled over his own feet. His strong, burly shoulders were hunched forward in submission, and he was incapable of standing upright.

I fumed. How dare he shirk his responsibilities! When Clarence returned to the house, I tried to calm myself and confront him.

"Where were you last night?"

"Just out with friends," Clarence said, sounding indifferent.

"You know you didn't do any of your chores, and I had to do them all for you?" Anger boiled out of me, and I could barely speak in even tones.

"I knew someone else would do it, either you or one of the field hands. That's what they're paid to do."

"Don't you even care that others are doing the work that is your responsibility? You are taking advantage of me and everyone else on this farm. You are incredibly selfish, and I won't have it."

"I'm not selfish. I just hate it here."

"What?" I raged, not believing his attitude. "This is your home. One day you and your brother will own this farm, and you must learn to take care of it. Ernie wants to update all of our outdated equipment, and he is going to need your help to run the finances and care for the property." I paused to get control of my anger. "I can't believe you hate our home. Our land. Your mother and I wanted this as your inheritance."

"I don't care. I never knew my mother, so she has no power over me. I don't want a life of constant work and worry like you have. I want more. I want to move to Milwaukee."

A thick silence grew between us like a poison slowly penetrating our space. "How long have you been thinking of this?" I calmly asked.

Clarence gathered himself and continued. "I'm just not interested in farming. I have a high school education and I like working with numbers. I could get a good job away from here, maybe become an accountant. They make thirty dollars a week. Molly said her uncle could get me into a training program to qualify for jobs in business."

I stopped listening after Clarence mentioned Molly because I knew I had no power to influence his thinking. A young man in love cannot be convinced his father has any ideas that measure up to those of his girlfriend. I walked away and left him alone, grieved at his overtaken heart.

CLARENCE

"Let's get out of here and go have some fun!" I shouted to my buddy, Sammy, who was working in the barn on a nearby farm.

"I'll be done in a half hour. Can you wait?"

"Of course."

I was driving my father's new Model T that Ernie had convinced him we needed. Thank heavens for Ernie, who kept my father up to date. If it wasn't for him, we would still be farming with sickles and rusty old pitchforks, requiring enough manual labor to run us all into the ground. At least we had a modern car.

Waiting for Sammy, I started to relax. After the fight with my father, I needed to get away and forget about how he was always on me. I may have been a little harsh with him, blurting out my plans for Milwaukee, but he needed to know how I felt.

Once Sammy finished work, we went to Pete's, our favorite hangout. We entered the shadowy room and took our seats at the bar. When Pete's first opened, its bar was just a large slab of wood balanced on two barrels. Now the deep-stained wood had been polished to a high gloss and protected by layers of shellac. Hand-carved legs with carved, ornate figures replaced the original barrels and behind the bar were muted, colored bottles of liquor and a varied selection of beers. Everybody knew everybody.

"It looks like you fellows need a little encouragement

from the Girl in the Moon," Peter said, referring to the beer company's logo. He pointed to the drawing of a girl sitting on a crescent-shaped moon, wearing what looked like a ringmaster costume.

"You got that right," I said, enjoying the familiarity of the bar's owner. We took a swig from our bottles and began our usual conversation. "I don't know how much longer I can continue living with my dad," I complained, remembering the anger I felt toward my father earlier in the day. "He is driving me crazy, and now he wants me to find a way to work happily with Ernie. We're going to modernize our farm and try all the new stuff Ernie learned at school. Can you believe that?"

"Modernizing the farm is a good idea," said Sammy. "I don't want to milk cows and bale hay for the rest of my life either, but I don't see you and Ernie working together."

"That's for sure," I said. "Ernie and I get along, but I want nothing to do with the farm, and he loves it."

Complaining was our favorite pastime, along with drinking beer, talking about girls, and dreaming about a future away from Brandon. "You are luckier than I am," Sammy said, taking another gulp from his bottle. "At least you have options and ideas. I don't know what I want to do or if I'm capable of doing anything else."

"I know I'm capable of much more than what my father thinks I am. He wants me to be just like him and do what he has done all his life. That's his definition of a good life, but I want to work with my brain, not my hands."

"I would love a career in business," Sammy said, "but I don't have someone like Molly to get me connected."

"Molly's great. I will be successful when I get out of here. Back in high school my favorite classes were math, and I was good at solving for X."

Sammy's attitude toward a life of farming coincided with mine. It was just too much work for such little reward. His dad, like mine, was a hard worker but had no vision for the future. Living in a small farmhouse with a coal-burning stove for cooking and an outhouse with a crescent-shaped moon on the door was not my idea of the good life. I wanted Sammy to confirm these thoughts.

Taking a large draw from my Miller High Life, I told Sammy about the latest argument with my father and how he walked out of the room when I mentioned Molly.

"You mean he didn't yell at you?" Sammy asked, now joining me with his own bottle of Miller's.

"He just blew up. I told him I wanted to be an accountant even though I'm not sure if I even like accounting. I just want to get out of here, and if I don't like accounting, I will find something I do like."

"I'm with you on that front," Sammy said. "Whatever it takes to get out of here."

"Thanks for listening."

Sammy and I stayed at the bar for a few hours until I left to go to Molly's. She lived on the outskirts of town in a new home recently built by her parents. Natural materials created a Craftsman look, popular in new construction. A shallow gable roof with visible beams covered a large porch looking onto the street. When Molly saw me, she waved from the corner of the porch and my mood lightened. All thoughts of my earlier argument dissipated.

"How was work today?" I asked.

"Pretty boring," a disinterested Molly responded. "Mr. Toll is so old and out of touch. He thinks we're still in the horse and buggy days." Molly folded her arms and walked to a corner of the porch.

I felt a growing concern as I followed her gaze. "All the more reason we have to get out of here as soon as possible. Let's talk."

For me, Molly was the realization of my dreams. She was beautiful, but not in a Gibson girl way; rather, she possessed a natural glow and an earthy beauty. She smiled with her eyes, radiating a warmth that drew people to her and sent chills up my spine. Like me, she had blonde hair and blue eyes but was delicate and graceful in her movements. She had that thing: when you talked to her, you felt like you were the most important person in her life. It was that "thing" that made me love her.

"Can you get me in touch with your uncle, the accountant, about a possible training program?" I asked. "I'm good with numbers and willing to study and learn new skills. I have experience in managing money. At work, Mr. Hazen sometimes asks me for ideas on how he can sell more cheese."

Molly looked away, her eyes growing cloudy as she shifted her gaze to some distant object.

"I don't know if my uncle can help."

"What do you mean? We talked about this before." My beer-laden stomach rumbled as waves of nausea crept up my throat, adding anxiety to my already troubled mind.

Molly stumbled over her words. "I think . . . Well, most of the people in his office have more. I mean, they went to college to learn accounting."

"I plan to get more training, maybe go to college. I'm inexperienced now, but I am a quick learner." I looked directly at Molly, but she refused to make eye contact.

"Well . . ." she said, sounding even more hesitant. "It takes a lot of training to be an accountant. I'm not sure you would like it."

"Molly, why can't you look at me? This has nothing to do with your uncle, does it?"

"Well . . ." Molly turned slowly to face me, her voice trailed off as she spoke. "My uncle isn't really the issue."

My heart sank to my stomach. "Then what is the issue? I thought we agreed that the two of us would move to Milwaukee together. I want it to happen soon."

Molly hesitated again before saying, "I'm not so sure."

"What do you mean you're not so sure?" I was angry and scared at the same time, going from disbelief to defiance. "You told me you wanted to get away and live in a big city."

Molly's eyes filled with tears while the rest of her body was rigid with tension, save for the muscles of her chin, which quivered. Her speech was soft, almost inaudible, but she managed to speak.

"I know what I said, but I'm not sure it can happen with you. I'm so sorry."

"What do you mean, you're sorry?" I retorted. "We are together in this plan. I know it, and I know you want it too."

"Maybe I did once, but things change, and I changed. I want something else now. With someone else."

My world shut down. My energy seeped out of my body and got pushed aside like an unwelcome obstacle. Molly didn't cherish, care, or love me. When did she decide to shatter my life? Where did this come from?

I drove home, struggling with my feelings. Molly raided my heart and took away my future, but I still loved her. We had a plan, now I had nothing. If I moved to Milwaukee, she would miss me and come to her senses. She would want me back, but I would grow hard, not take her back immediately, even though in the end, I would forgive her. Our plan could still happen. This was only a minor setback.

I arrived at home. My father was waiting for me, and I told him my plan to move.

"You can't move to Milwaukee." My father's anger was palpable.

"Yes, I can, and I will."

"At least wait until Ernie gets home and we can work something out. Summer is approaching and I'll need help with the crops. Have you been drinking again?"

"No, I have not," I raged at my father. "I can move out when I want. You don't get it, Dad. Ernie loves it here. I don't. The farm will be fine without me. You can hire some help since I didn't actually do a lot of work anyway."

"That's the first realistic thing you've said: you don't do a lot. But you're the one who doesn't get it. This farm is my lifeblood, and it should be yours as well."

"Well, it isn't."

"Clarence," my father said, trying to stay calm. "We have been on this land for more than fifty years and it has been good to us. You can't leave; we're family."

"Dad, I can't change how I feel. I need to get away from here and start a new life. Molly and I broke up and I need something new. It is stifling being here."

"Is this about Molly?"

"No, Dad," I lied. "Ernie will be home soon, and he shares your love of farming. He will take care of things."

"Let's talk about this tomorrow after we've had a good night's sleep. Things will look different."

"I don't think so. I love you but I have to leave."

My chin sank into the palm of my hand as I rested my elbow on the ledge of the only window in my single-room apartment above the fruit district in Milwaukee. I surveyed the rain-soaked street below and watched people scurry around, jumping over puddles and splashing dirty water on the hems of their once clean clothes. Some people were shouting while they ran to catch the nearby streetcar, but the muddy, messy ground slowed their progress. Directly below my window was a fruit market with its bright-yellow awnings stretching into the street, providing shade for the crates of fresh produce under its protective covering. I couldn't see the stacks of Macintosh apples, Green Gage plums, or Robinson strawberries, but the smell of the fruit drifted into my window and made me nostalgic for the apple orchards of my home miles away. Horse-drawn carts, laden with the bounty of a good harvest, traversed the rain-soaked street below me; the squashing sound of hooves sinking into puddles brought back memories of my youth. I glanced down at the paint-chipped wood of my windowsill and saw little bugs creeping out of the cracks, looking for the fruit they smelled but could not find. They were lost, misguided by the enticing smell of sweetness, but their search, like mine, was in vain. I was a long way from the open farmland and simple existence I once had, but it was what I chose.

Feeling lonely and somewhat unsure of myself, I moved away from the window and thought about the decision I made. I never wanted to live on the farm my entire life, but was this move rebellion against my father or a reaction to Molly's rejection? I reached for a piece of paper on my nightstand and began writing my thoughts, a list of pros and cons and how I got to where I was. I liked a little self-examination.

Not satisfied with my writing skills, I decided to call home. My boarding house had one phone per floor, and I called long distance to talk to Ernie and Dad.

I dropped in my coins, rang for the operator, and connected with Ernie. After our hello, he started filling me in. "The crops are in and we're using some of the hybrids I learned about in school. With all the new research I learned, we'll be the best farm in the state."

"That's great." I ignored his exuberance. "Is Dad around?"

"I'll go get him."

"Tell him to hurry up. I'm running out of quarters."

"Hello," my dad said in his usual deadpan voice. "How are you?"

"Great," I replied. "I thought I'd call to say hello before going to work at the fruit market."

"Do you make enough money to support yourself?"

"Sure," I replied. This conversation was the same every time, so I tried to change the subject. "I've met a new friend who is a carpenter, and he's trying to convince me to join him tonight for a meeting with some of the guys he works with."

"Good, I'm glad you met some new people," my dad said, though he sounded uninterested. "I have to go now and fix dinner. I'll talk more next time."

My father hung up. I realized we had the same conversation—or lack of a conversation—each time I called.

John, my new friend, saw me in the hallway with my head slumped over my chest.

"Was that a bad phone call?" he asked.

"Just typical family stuff." I gathered myself together and tucked my problems into the back compartment of my brain.

"I'm going to a union meeting tonight," John said. "Do you want to join me?"

"I don't think I can. I'm not a member."

"It doesn't matter. They're looking for new people. There are a lot of job opportunities in the trades today."

"I certainly need a good job. I can barely support myself with the job at the fruit market." I tried to sound enthused.

"If you want a good job, you could get training and join the United Brotherhood of Carpenters trade union."

"What's that?" I asked.

"They're a growing force in organizing laborers in Milwaukee. Most other trades work ten or twelve-hour days, but eight hours is the standard length of a carpenter's workday."

"That sounds good to me," I said.

"It is good, and it pays well. The guys who are building the Brumder mansion on Wisconsin Avenue want me to go because they're going to discuss collective bargaining. They have a guest speaker coming. He's a politician who wants to bring some new ideas into the labor unions."

This was all new to me, as I didn't know anything about the Brumder mansion, or why John was involved. Neither did I know anything about collective bargaining. I first asked him about the Brumder mansion.

"You should see it." John's excitement was becoming infectious. "The rich people in the city think it's healthier to live away from Lake Michigan. This newspaper man built a three-story red-brick mansion about a twenty-minute buggy ride from downtown."

"Are you sure? What a crazy idea! How can anyone not want to live along the lake! The cool air, the peace and quiet, the swimming, the fishing, I would want it all."

"Well, believe it." John smiled at me. "I've been working there for the past year. It needed a lot of carpentry to finish the details, and you should see the craftsmanship of some of the German immigrants. Just incredible." John looked at his calloused hands. "My hands look like a baby's bottom compared to theirs."

Later that night, John and I went to a meeting at Turner

Hall, a historic building primarily used as a gymnasium but also seconded as a meeting hall. Cathedral-like stained-glass windows framed the outside walls. Political slogans of Turner's philosophy, a progressive movement of the 1800s, were incorporated into the stained-glass design. The inside walls were covered with murals done by artists depicting historic events and were considered some of the best panoramic paintings of their time.

John and I walked into the great hall. "Look at the crowd in here," I said, amazed. "Everyone is smoking and drinking and speaking a language filled with guttural and nasal noise. It sounds pretty harsh."

"Haven't you ever heard German before?" John asked. "Some of these guys have only been here a short time, so they don't speak English."

"Remember," I said, looking at John. "I'm a farm boy used to open spaces and clean air. I feel like I'm breathing coal into my lungs, the smoke is so thick."

"Actually, this room is usually used for gymnastics, so there's no smoking during training, but for meetings, those rules do not apply. You can see they pushed all the equipment to the side so they would have room for the assembly."

The sheer size of the room dwarfed the people inside and made me feel small and insignificant. There were rings and ropes hanging from the ceiling. Additional apparatuses, pummel horses, parallel and horizontal bars, and mats for tumbling were pushed against the wall to create space for the meeting. I was entering a world where strength and skill were built, and I wanted to be a part of it.

"Wait until the meeting starts," John said, bringing me back to the reason we were there. "If you want to be a carpenter and be a part of this organization, you will need a union card because, without it, you have no trade."

"Why not?" I asked. "Can't I just learn the skill and get a job? Especially if they need carpenters?"

"It doesn't work that way. The union negotiates collective agreements for their workers, and you will get better wages, shorter working hours, better training, health plans, and a lot more. This union is going to make us great, and Milwaukee is at the forefront of the movement. If tonight's guest speaker, Victor Berger, wins the November election, he will be the first socialist congressman in the US government. You need to hear him."

"I like the sound of this," I said.

The room went quiet as the union president approached the podium. He began his introduction: "I would like to introduce tonight's speaker, a man you are all familiar with, a founding member of the Socialist Party of America. He is an advocate of the trade union-oriented politics, and after the November elections, he will be the first socialist to serve in the United States Congress. Let's welcome the future congressman of Wisconsin's fifth congressional district, Victor Berger."

A cheer went up from the crowd as a short, stocky man walked up to the podium. He looked uncomfortable in his role as speaker, and once he began his talk, it was obvious this was not a platform where he excelled. He had a heavy German accent, and his voice did not project well throughout the auditorium. I suspected he was better at behind-the-scenes operations rather than being the spokesperson for the movement. Nonetheless, he had the attention of the crowd, and everyone was intent on listening to what he had to say.

I liked the speech. Berger's ideas about unions and a collective society resonated with me, and I thought it could be applied to farming as well. In an environment where everyone was equal and each farm worked as a part of the whole, there was no need to worry about "who had the best farm." Ernie would hate it, but I could work under that system; that is, if I ever went back to farming.

"Did you enjoy the speech?" John asked on our walk home. He looked a little tipsy after an evening filled with beer and camaraderie.

I thought for a minute before saying, "I think Berger is on to something. He obviously has a big ego, but I think he could influence a lot of people."

"I heard he has a terrible temper and has trouble dealing with anyone holding a contrary opinion," John countered.

"That doesn't bother me. I like his ideas. I think I will discuss them with my father and brother. My dad may agree, but my brother never will. I need to patch up my relationship with my dad before I try to convince him of this new way of looking at things."

When I got back to the boarding house, one of the other boarders came up to me with a message. It was from Ernie. "Urgent, call home," the message said.

I picked up the phone and called my brother.

"Hello." Ernie's voice was low and shaking.

"What's wrong? I got a message to call you."

"There's been an accident." Ernie's voice was so low I could barely hear him.

"What do you mean? What kind of accident?"

"We were working in the barn and Dad wanted to talk to me about something. He looked worried and tired, so we decided to put the horse away first and then talk."

"Did he want to talk about me? Lately, we haven't been getting along."

"I don't think so," Ernie's voice was tight and restrained.

I continued, "I was just about to call him with some new ideas. I wanted to patch up our relationship."

"That can't happen now," said Ernie. "Dad wasn't thinking clearly because he walked up to Junior—you know, our old horse—and approached him from the back. Junior reacted."

"You don't mean he approached from his blind spot? Dad knows better than that."

"I guess he didn't realize where he was because that is exactly what he did. Junior just reacted and kicked Dad in the chest. I heard the smack of the impact when Junior's hoof hit his chest and I knew it was bad."

"How is he?"

Ernie was silent. I could hear a tea kettle whistling in the background, insects humming their annoying songs, and the night call of a wild animal but I could not hear Ernie's voice, only the muffled sound of crying.

Finally, Ernie choked on his words. "He died instantly. You have to come home."

———————◆———————

Ernie and I sat and stared into the empty room of our childhood home. The room still echoed with Dad's voice, but what was familiar in the past was now vague and distant. Even the bright sun outside couldn't penetrate the black fog separating me from everything I once knew.

"It's a sad day," I said to Ernie, who looked ghostlike.

Ernie remained silent so I continued. "The funeral was beautiful but I'm glad everybody is gone. Being around our family and Dad's other friends makes me sad. It feels good to get away."

He shot a bitter look at me. "That's what you always do, Clarence. Whenever you're needed, you just want to get away."

"Wait a minute," I said, sitting up rigidly. "Dad and I may not have had a perfect relationship, but I loved him and never wanted anything like this to happen." My old anger flared up with a wrath that tested the boundaries of my loyalty. I turned away and started to leave.

"Are you going to stay in Brandon for a while, or do you need to get back to the excitement of a big city?" Ernie said sarcastically.

"That's not fair. I did not leave so I could go and have a good time. I wanted to start a new career, away from farming. I'm not like you."

"Do you have any intention of helping out around here?"

"I will stay for a little while and then decide what to do. I met some people in Milwaukee with interesting ideas, some of which would be good for the farm."

"We don't have to talk about it now," Ernie turned compliant. "It can wait."

"Okay," I said as I walked into my old room and fell into my bed. I tried to sleep but a carousel of memories played in my mind. I couldn't relax. The fulfillment of my dad's dream versus the excitement of a new life played over and over in my head. I was torn and didn't know what to do. When the carousel finally slowed and allowed my mind to quiet, I drifted into a restless sleep.

The next morning, I made breakfast for Ernie, hoping to talk about my new ideas. I wasn't sure how he would respond, but I wanted to at least test the waters to get his reaction.

"Before Dad's accident," I started, "a friend brought me to hear a speech by a socialist politician who has done a lot of work with local unions. My friend is in the Carpenter's Union, and he thinks I should join."

"Go ahead," said Ernie. "It's your life."

I ignored his disinterest. "The politician talked about collective bargaining to improve working conditions and share profits. He was speaking to carpenters, but I could see an application to farming as well."

Ernie was quiet, but I could tell he was thinking about how to respond. "That may sound like a good idea," he said, "but what about someone who wants to work independently? If I work harder than someone else, I don't want to give them any of my profits."

"But why should we compete with each other?" I continued. "Each farm would specialize in a different crop and work together for the benefit of everyone. Profits would be divided equally."

"Are you crazy?" The anger in his voice cut through the air and electrified the room. "Dad spent his entire life building this farm and I went to school just to learn improved methods. We own this land, and I will never give it up or share it with someone else."

"I never said give up the land!" I shouted. "I just think we should form our own community. I think we would profit from working together."

Ernie's face became red with rage as he gritted his teeth and clenched his fists. "I haven't studied all these years just so others can steal my ideas and take advantage of my knowledge. Let them go to school and learn the way I did."

Realizing this discussion was going to escalate into a major argument, I backed away. "This isn't a good time to talk. We're still in shock about losing Dad. We'll talk later."

A week passed with Ernie and I coexisting in the same

house, but with minimal interaction. Friends and other family members were still bringing food for us as if we were helpless orphans who couldn't take care of ourselves. Molly came over to offer condolences, but it only made me more miserable.

Finally, we met with Uncle Herman, Dad's attorney, to complete the paperwork and transfer the title of the farm. Ernie and I needed to learn how to work together despite our differences, but it was going to take time. We entered Uncle Herman's office, both of us solemn and awkwardly polite to each other.

"Welcome," Uncle Herman greeted us, clearly hiding nervousness behind his smile. After he itemized everything in the estate, we proceeded to the reading of the will.

"Very unusual," Uncle Herman said. "Henry's accident occurred just after signing this new statement. If I could have foreseen the future, I might have advised him differently."

"What is unusual?" I asked.

"When I wrote your father's will many years ago, he stated he had no debts, and all of his possessions should be divided equally between the two of you." Uncle Herman paused for a long time before continuing. "Two weeks ago, Henry came into my office and said he wanted to make some changes to his will. Clarence had gone to Milwaukee and was no longer interested in farming. He wanted Ernie to have the farm. Instead of changing everything in the will, I advised Henry to sign over the deed to the property thus giving the title to Ernie. My thinking was Henry would probably change his mind, and it would be easier to change the deed rather than write a new will. I never thought this would actually happen."

"You mean Ernie gets the farm? I'm left out?" My face felt hot.

Ernie's disbelief mirrored mine and he turned to me with an expression of shock. "You have to know I had no idea Dad was going to do this." Ernie chocked on his words.

I turned to Uncle Herman. "Is there anything else you can tell me about my father?"

"Your father loved both of you boys but felt Clarence preferred city living and pursuing his new interests. He decided to let Ernie have the farm. We signed the papers just a week before his accident, and now I wonder if he would have made that decision had he known he had such a short time to live."

"I don't believe it!" Livid, I jumped out of my chair. "Dad and I had our differences, but never did I think he would treat me this way. I grew up on this farm just like Ernie, so half of it should be mine. Is his signature on the deed legal? The will states half of everything goes to me."

Uncle Herman was having difficulty making eye contact and was obviously uncomfortable. "It is legal. You can contest the title, but you will have to take legal action against your brother. The courts will decide the outcome. You would have to show undue influence, fraud, or testamentary capacity, which means you're saying your father was not of sound mind when he signed the document."

"Clarence, I didn't know about this change," Ernie said. "Dad never said a thing to me. I think we should go home and talk about it."

"This is your doing," I said, berating my brother. "You and Dad never wanted me around and I never got a chance to tell him my ideas. You got what you always wanted, and now you don't have to worry about me interfering with your grand plan. I hope you're happy. I am no longer a part of this family."

I stormed out of Uncle Herman's office in a rage. I didn't care if Ernie knew about the deed transfer or not. He manipulated our father into giving him the farm and leaving me out in the cold. I needed aggressive action; I wanted what was mine.

I took the Model T back to our house—now Ernie's house—and left Ernie to find his own way home. I did not want to face him until I had more control over my anger and had time to formulate a plan. He was not going to get away with this.

Once home, I packed my bags and got ready to leave for the train station. The realization hit me that I might never be back again. I wanted to take something, a remembrance of my father, so his memory would always stay with me. I went into his desk drawer and grabbed the gold coin I knew he kept there.

The coin was special to my father, as it had been given to him by *his* father and was a token of luck and good fortune. It didn't bring him much luck, but it was especially satisfying to me because I knew Ernie loved that coin.

I went back to Milwaukee still raging, and sat in my single room overlooking the fruit market. People were scurrying around, packing crates, and loading trucks, but everything in my life had changed. The farm I couldn't wait to escape now became my fixation. Originally, I left because I wanted the city. I didn't want the farm. But once I lost it, getting the farm back became the focus of my life.

Time passed but my anger never diminished, nor could I accept the fact that my inheritance went completely to my brother. I tried to think about my new life, but all I could do was obsess over getting what was rightfully mine, the farm. I hired an attorney, who sent a letter to Ernie and Uncle Herman contesting the legality of the new deed. I specifically instructed my lawyer not to say anything negative about my father. My problem was with Ernie, not my father.

Months passed before we got a court date. I had not talked

to Ernie since the reading of the will, and now we were sitting on opposing sides of a courtroom, waiting for a ruling. Finally, the judge read the claim.

A signed quitclaim deed overrides a will because the property covered by the deed is not part of the estate. The deed needs to be notarized, and it was. Everything was done legally and stands as is.

I did not speak to Ernie, and he just stared at the judge triumphantly. My shoulders collapsed into my chest and disappointment arrived as sadness. I got up and left the room.

I returned to Milwaukee, trying to put my life back together. Getting an apprenticeship in carpentry helped, but I worked unreasonably hard. My body ached and my hands became red and raw. Sleep evaded me and I was miserable.

Several months later, coming home one night, I found another urgent message, this time from Uncle Herman. I tensed, remembering the last time I received such a message. I picked up the phone and dialed.

"Hello," Uncle Herman answered.

"This is Clarence," I said. "You wanted to talk to me?"

"Yes, I'm afraid I have some bad news." The voice on the other end of the phone went silent and I felt my life pause. I knew something dreadful happened. Uncle Herman finally spoke. "Your brother, Ernie, was found at the bottom of the septic system on the farm. He did not survive the fall."

"You mean he died? That can't be."

"Nobody is sure what happened, but he must have fallen and hit his head. He had been drinking."

I was disoriented, like a camera flashed in my eyes, blinding me until everything slowly came into focus. "What are you talking about?" I said. "Ernie doesn't drink, and he would never wander around by that stinky pit."

"Your brother has been different these last few months, and he lost a lot of his optimistic nature. He withdrew from almost everyone around him and started to drink. I don't think he ever got over the loss of your father or, for that matter, you."

"What do I need to do?" I asked.

"You need to come home and take care of the final arrangements. You're his only heir."

"I have no home, if you remember correctly."

"The farm now belongs to you," Uncle Herman said.

"This is not what I want," I said. "Ernie and I had our differences, but we're family and he is all I have left." I felt sick and tried to choke down the bitter fluids rising from my stomach.

"Clarence," said my uncle softly. "Nobody wanted this to happen. We all thought eventually you and Ernie would work things out, but fate intervened. I'm sorry. Call me when you get here."

I packed my bags and prepared to leave Milwaukee one more time. I took a last look at the fruit vendors below my window and remembered how excited I was my first day, watching the bustling activity on the street. Horse-drawn wagons piled high with boxes of fruit lined the street and everything was vibrant and new. Today the workers seemed tired, listless, and the sounds of panting horses was replaced by the rumbling engines of pick-up trucks.

I reached into my pocket and pressed the gold coin into the palm of my hand, thinking about my father. Its smoothness comforted me and bolstered my confidence so I could face the grief ahead. I did not have a token to remember my twin brother, but there would always be a voice in the back of my head, a whispering sound, connecting us. We both pulled on each other's orbit, sometimes colliding, but sorrow was now the voice that filled my head. I wanted to remember him, to find a means to keep him alive in my head and in my heart. I was in the habit of writing my thoughts on random scraps of paper, but I needed something more organized, like a diary. I would start one when I got to the farm.

———

As I approached my childhood home, everything looked the same yet different. The wind was strong, coming out of the north, curling around tree branches, and distorting their upright posture. The sky was a mass of gray clouds descending to the horizon, blocking any warmth from the sun, and preventing shafts of light from reaching the fields. The aroma of alfalfa, cows, barnyard animals, and manure that once filled the air was gone. This landscape, this farm, was once so familiar but today it appeared remote, cold, and unwelcoming. I now owned all of it.

As I entered the house, I felt the ghosts of my family watching me with critical eyes. Chilling sensations filled each room, accusing me, assaulting me, demanding to know how this tragedy could happen. I could barely breathe without taking in the misery that had befallen my family. I had to leave.

"I'm glad to see you," started Uncle Herman as he approached me with a friendly handshake.

"I wish I could be here under better circumstances," I replied, looking down at my dirty shoes tracking in mud from the farm into the tidy lawyer's office. "I want to know what happened to Ernie. He couldn't simply wander around and fall into the septic pit."

"Have a seat, Clarence," Uncle Herman motioned to a chair. "I'll tell you what I know."

Uncle Herman started, "Ernie was not the same after your

father died. He became depressed, but there was something else, something I can't put a label on. Several people saw him walking on Main Street in town. When they called to him, he didn't respond or acknowledge them in any way. Outwardly, he wore the same weathered clothes and farmer's hat, but he looked thin, shuffled as he walked and made no eye contact. Your friend Sammy tried to talk to him, but Ernie just walked away as if Sammy was as invisible as a ghost."

"Did you talk to Ernie about any of this?" I asked.

"Not at first, until I ran into Sammy a second time at the hardware store. He asked again if I knew what was wrong with Ernie. I told him I didn't know anything, but I would check."

"I drove out to the farm the next day and saw Ernie working in the barn. He was friendly and talked about building a new barn, like his father had wanted. After a few minutes, he lost his train of thought and could no longer concentrate on what he was saying. His conversation turned to talking about school and not going back, and then he switched back to talking about building the barn. He couldn't look me in the eyes. He was nervous. I asked him about seeing friends or going into town and he said he hadn't been in Brandon in months. I tried to get him to say more, but he insisted he hadn't been anywhere near Brandon and preferred to stay on the farm."

"I'm not surprised Ernie preferred life on the farm," I added, "but he was not a liar and he never suffered from blackouts. If he said he didn't go into town, he must have believed it."

"You're right," replied my uncle. "I went to talk to my brother Augie—your uncle—and he, too, felt that something was wrong with Ernie. He told me of an incident where Ernie walked to another farm but had no memory of being there and denied that it happened. Augie said it was like he had amnesia.

Ernie couldn't remember where he'd been or who he had talked to."

I sunk into the chair and a massive headache started at the nape of my neck and circled around to my forehead. My brother was always the stable one in the family. I was the screwup who caused problems and then left. Uncle Herman was not describing the Ernie that I knew.

"Why didn't you call me?"

"Clarence, you know why I didn't call. You and Ernie weren't speaking, and I didn't think you could help in any way."

"That's not true. He was still my brother, my family, and I could have done something."

"Maybe you're right, given what happened."

"Do you actually know what happened?"

"I was told he fell into the wastewater system and hit his head on the way down, nothing more. The police thought he was drinking, but I doubt it. Whatever was going on in Ernie's mind caused him to be careless, or maybe he just didn't know where he was. It will always be a mystery."

Tears formed in my eyes as I left my uncle's office. There must be more to the story than what I had been told. Ernie did not walk around unaware of where he was, nor did he ignore people. He was driven by his ideas and plans and was governed by logic. The brother I loved was not the person who recklessly fell into a pit.

Could I have somehow been responsible? I disrupted the fabric of our family with my attitude, always arguing and never compromising. A black shadow followed me back to the farm I now owned. Ernie's tragic death would haunt me forever.

KIM

ROUND THREE

MARCH 8, 2009

"Why am I putting myself through this drug-fest?" I ask Dr. Williams, my second opinion doctor and supposedly the best Lymphoma specialist in the state. "Isn't it a foregone conclusion that I have a low probability of beating this cancer?"

"You're receiving the recommended treatment and it's your best chance for remission," he answers.

"That's what I've been told," I say, disillusioned with this standard response. "I would like to know about my prognosis."

Dr. Williams takes command of the conversation. He is a tall, erect man with a military-like presence and an authoritative voice. Warm and fuzzy is not his style, but he is a person people would follow into battle because of the sheer dominance of his character. He wears gun-metal gray glasses to match the deep, steely gray of his eyes. His skin is monochromatic, cold, and dry like parchment with a rough-looking texture. He's all business, no small talk, and wants to move quickly through the discussion. He doesn't look as if he was ever a little boy who loved playing in the dirt.

"What have you already been told?" asks the drill sergeant doctor.

His presence is intimidating, so I speak rapidly, without filters. I give him the medical history I've been told covering the past few weeks and wait for his response.

"It's true T-Cell is more complicated than B-Cell, but the treatment is the same."

Overcoming my fear of intimidation, I gather my strength. "I would like to know about my prognosis. What life span can I expect? I mean, how long will I have any quality of life?"

There is no hesitation or softening from Dr. Williams. "We have only seen a few cases at this hospital, but the survival rate is not high. Few make it longer than a year after treatment."

This news rolls over me like a slow-moving tank, painful and impossible to stop. Dr. Williams sounds like he is reciting out of a textbook using long, laborious phrases and a flat intonation pattern. He delivers his message without fanfare. A politician he is not.

"Does anybody survive beyond the chemotherapy?" I ask, looking for a silver lining somewhere.

"Of course," he says, softening a little. "There are no guarantees, but some people go through a bone marrow transplant. It's a difficult procedure and I do not recommend it for you."

"Why not?"

"We do not administer it to older patients. The long-term results of the treatment do not justify the risk."

"So, I'm old."

"No, you are not old. It's just that the procedure and recovery are difficult. Some patients don't make it through the process."

"I see."

Each word Dr. Williams utters is another nail in my coffin. I retreat to my inner self and slip into the silent, dark part of my mind, turning off external stimulation. This is usually the point where Mark takes over the conversation and allows me to be absent, but even he cannot digest this painful news. A few weeks ago, I was thinking death was a way out of my misery, but now that I am face-to-face with the reality of it, I find uncertainty creeping into my once self-confident decision.

My mind drifts. After reading the account of Clarence and Ernie in Clarence's diary, their loss has haunted me. Like Ernie, I've always felt that I was governed by logic, and yet I've fallen into a great pit. Like Clarence, I've lost someone I cannot get back, and it haunts me even in ways I do not see. I am both brothers.

I hear my name mentioned and snap back into the moment. Mark is in deep conversation with the doctor, standing by his desk. I know Mark is angry; I can see it in his body language. His face is blank, his body tilts forward, and his arms are folded across his chest. It is a defensive posture, ready to accept blows. The doctor is more upright, on the attack with his imposing dominance and authoritarian manner. The only portion of the conversation I hear is, "We've done all we can, I'm sorry."

Those seven words, constructed in a simple sentence, spoken with finality, cut through me with an ache in my stomach that rocks back and forth. I convinced myself that I wanted death because it would take me away from the pain of missing Billy, but what's ahead for me now? A fiery pit or a castle in the sky? Will death bring relief or surprise? No matter what, I am afraid.

The ride home is painful. I watch the landscape roll by as I drift into a semi-conscious sleep. Darkness surrounds me, and only a shimmering glow in the distance is visible. I strain to see what is held by the bright light, and as I get closer, I recognize my son. He is playing baseball and I call to him, but he doesn't listen. I watch him but he seems unaware. As I approach the light, he retreats. It is one of those lucid dreams where I know I'm dreaming but feel I am experiencing real life. No matter what I do, I can't move fast enough to get to my son. My arms hang loose by my side and my feet can't propel me forward. I try to call to him, but my voice has no sound.

"Kim, are you all right?"

I snap back and look at Mark, who is struggling to keep his eyes on the road.

"You were mumbling and looked like you were in the middle of a battle," he says.

"Maybe," I reply as I bow my head and look down at my trembling hands. "I can't go through this anymore. I feel it's hopeless."

"You will not give up, and I am not giving up on you." Mark is adamant.

Looking at the passing countryside once again, I can't shake the fear building inside me. Dr Williams delivered a knockout punch and I know it's time for me to prepare for the end. I tell myself I will not turn into a vegetable, but face death with a sound mind and dignity.

———————

I almost didn't make it to my third round of chemotherapy, not because I was giving up on the treatment, but because of the ever-unpredictable Wisconsin weather. Spring is just around the corner with new foliage budding, crocuses and daffodils peeking out of the recently thawed ground, but that is not the case. The weatherman predicted a major storm with rain, snow, sleet, and maybe all three. And for once, he is right.

The storm is in full swing as we are leaving the house. The howling wind threatens to uproot me as I make my way to the snowy sidewalk. Ice pellets bounce off my winter coat, and I bow my head low and tuck my chin into my chest to avoid the sting of ice on my face. Mark walks ahead, clearing a path so I can follow in his newly imprinted footsteps. They lead to the detached garage, which is suddenly far away from the house.

"How are you doing?" Mark yells, his voice muffled and barely audible over the roar of the wind.

"I'm fine. Let's just get to the car and turn on the heat. My whole body is shaking."

Mark is also miserable. He doesn't have a waterproof winter jacket and is starting to get wet as well as cold. "Next time we buy a house," he says, "let's make sure it has an attached garage. I'm way past wanting to trudge through this weather."

Under my breath, I say, "If there is a next time."

Once in the garage, I brush the ice off my coat and get mad—mad at the weather, mad at Mark, mad at cancer, and most of all, mad at myself for being mad at everything. "There is nothing fun about this storm!" I shout. "It's not the white, fluffy stuff of my childhood dreams. I hate it."

"That's for sure," says Mark. "Next winter, we're becoming snowbirds."

"Sure," I say, not believing the discrepancy between what he says and what I feel is true. It saddens me.

We make it to the hospital despite the snow blowing and drifting across the highway.

"Welcome. I see you made it through the storm," Dr. Belmont says as we enter his office with our wet clothes and frozen faces.

"It certainly is miserable out there," says Mark. "I love a summer storm when it cleans the air and makes everything fresh, but this I can do without."

Dr. Belmont begins with his usual string of questions. "Were the side effects tolerable this time?"

"I still had trouble," I say. "The fog came five days after

treatment, but it was not as bad as the first time. I'm a little more functional.

"Have you spent time with the rest of your family?"

Mark quickly jumps into the conversation, saving me from answering. "Kim's voice has been affected by the treatment, and she can't talk normally." Mark looks to me for affirmation.

"In what way?" asks Dr. Belmont.

I nod to Mark but answer the question in my own words. "In order to say anything, I need to inhale deeply and then force the air over my vocal cords. That takes effort, so my conversations are brief and slow."

"Your family won't mind. They probably just want to spend time with you."

"Maybe." I pause, distracting myself by looking at the peaceful picture hanging on the wall. A young boy in dungarees and a straw hat is holding an oversized watering can, trying to water his flowers. The picture is sweet and nostalgic, but it does not relax me. I turn to Dr. Belmont and continue.

"I had another problem these last three weeks. I had vertigo and could not walk without support. I need help going to the bathroom, which is a big problem when it happens in the middle of the night."

"We have a pee bottle we can give you," Dr. Belmont says.

"I know about pee bottles. Do you have any idea how difficult it is to urinate into one of those when you are female and must lie flat? It cannot be done without spilling all over the bed. I don't think you know what it's like."

"No, I don't know what it's like, but it does help."

"I want a penis," I blurt out, shocking Dr. Belmont. His stunned expression and red face break through his anchorman demeanor. "I want to put it in the bottle and relieve myself without creating a septic tank of my bed."

Mark is trying desperately to hide the subtle smile spreading across his face but meeting with little success.

"I don't know what to tell you." Dr. Belmont chokes on his words. "You just have to tough it out because the treatment is working. The lump under your arm is gone, and I don't see enlarged lymph nodes any place else. Your body has accepted the treatment despite how it feels to you." He pauses to compose himself. "I can help you with the cancer, but you'll have to talk to a plastic surgeon about the other issue."

"I'll make that my next appointment," I say. "Thank you for indulging my sick sense of humor."

"No problem," says the doctor. "I've had tougher patients, but you're the first to request a penis as part of your treatment protocol."

After leaving the doctor's office, it's time for treatment. I take my place in The Chair, as I now call it, and wait for the nurse. The Chair has taken on a bipolar personality, quite apart from the perceived serenity of my first visit. The Chair symbolizes drugs that cause pain; it is the delivery system for fog, fatigue, and for these past three weeks, vertigo. But it is also the vehicle for sending the healing poison into my veins. I have mixed feelings about its benefits and confusion over how I want to continue.

Looking out the window at Lake Michigan, Mark smiles.

"What's so funny? I'm facing the end of my life, and you're laughing at me?"

"I can't help it," Mark says. "I never knew you had penis envy!"

I shake my head. "I totally lost it in there, didn't I?"

"I was happy to see a little of the old Kim come back," he says. "I'm not sure the doctor deserved your wrath, but it had to make you feel better."

"I think I was still upset from our visit to the lymphoma specialist. I've been miserable ever since."

"Dr. Williams was pessimistic and brutal. You can't let him get you down."

I close my eyes and think about what the rest of my life looks like. Before the cancer, Mark and I were barely speaking to each other, and now he is laughing at my weird sense of humor. We have not laughed together since Billy died, but we did have happier times, many shared experiences. I'll never forget our trip to Northern Vietnam and the rice paddies.

We were hiking across the wet rocks that formed a checkerboard pattern around rice paddies. The fields climbed up the mountainside in an engineering feat that probably existed for thousands of years. It was a beautiful sight to behold. The rocks were slippery, and I had a walking stick for balance, but Mark, the true adventurer, wore leather-soled street shoes and had nothing to help with stability. I was ahead of him with a guide when I heard a splash and knew someone had fallen into the dung-laden rice paddy. I sent a silent prayer up in the hopes it wasn't Mark.

Turning around I saw him sitting in the rice paddy, up to his waist in muck, hyperventilating. He spit out a string of obscenities even a sailor would find remarkable. The guides tried to help him stand, but he resisted and fell backwards like a giant fish struggling to get free. He finally made it out and we finished our hike, but not without a lot of profanity about how much he loved the place.

"I'm going home." Mark looked like Wile E. Coyote after being foiled by the roadrunner, his head ready to explode.

"How are you going to get there? We're in the middle of a rice paddy in Vietnam."

"Can't you call a taxi?"

I dissolved into a puddle of laughter, even though he was serious. "Where do you think we are? New York City?"

Mark did not think this was funny and mumbled something that I, thankfully, couldn't hear.

Thinking of this now, my inner smile grows, and I almost feel alive. It saddens me to think those days are gone.

"Why do you have a smile on your face?" Mark interrupts my musing.

Not realizing my smile was visible, I turn to Mark, thinking about the loving feelings we once shared. We are no longer those people. Things change and I am sitting in a chemo chair facing death. My mood shifts and when I look at Mark again, I don't see him. I see the eyes of my son, the hair of my son, the gleam of Billy's smile. I pause, tuck those memories away, and say, "I was just thinking of you falling in the rice paddy. It's still funny after all these years."

"Funny for you." Mark smiles.

When I get home, I decide to clean out my messy closets. My motive is to get organized and not leave a lot of loose ends for Mark to handle after I am gone. Reaching back to a shelf in the back of the closet, I find an old shoebox containing a treasure more valuable than my gold coin. I uncover my parents' love story. It must have gotten tucked away when Julie and I cleaned my father's house and we never bothered to look inside.

Blowing away multiple layers of dust, I open the box to find a stack of envelopes neatly wrapped with a red, white, and blue ribbon. Carefully untying the ribbon, I notice each envelope contains a letter inside written on thin paper. The envelopes are postmarked with the dates (1944–1945), a symbol of the US military, and a large *V*. These letters must be at least eighty years old and written during WWII. I examine some of the letters and each begins with "Dearest Lizzie." I can't believe it. These are letters from when my father was in the army.

The box also contained a picture of my father in a military uniform and my mother in a patriotic red, white, and blue ensemble. My parents are glowing with love and adoration and look so happy together. This does not fit with my memories of a father who was quick-tempered and strict and a mother who was subservient to him. I never thought they had a great marriage, but these letters show a great love. What happened to them? The pictures in Julie's scrapbook, taken years later, show my parents closed off from each other, separate and not touching, just like the way Mark and I look today.

THE GAUGERS

THE WAR

LIZZIE
1944

My mother yelled out the back door of our house, "Hey Lizzie, c'mon in. You got a letter!"

I was living with my parents, Clarence and Flossy, in Fox Point, a suburb of Milwaukee, while my husband, Fred, was overseas on the European front. I tried to help around the house to earn my keep, but my current task of picking strawberries for dinner wasn't entirely successful since most of the strawberries ended up in my mouth.

I flew into the house in a wave of excitement. "Sorry about dinner tonight. I ate the strawberries."

"That's all right." My mother smiled. "It's far more important you look at this V-mail and see what's new."

"I'm sure it's from Fred," I said. "The only other person who writes from overseas is Carl, and he wrote the family a few days ago. I'd be surprised if my brother sent another letter so soon!"

Fred and I married in September 1940, the same month the government enacted the Selective Service Act, the first peacetime draft in history. The probability of war was high, and I constantly worried about Fred having to go overseas and fight in Europe. His brother, Jim, was 1-A because he was younger, not working in a war industry, and not married. Fred could also be drafted but he was married, head of a household but had no children. As it turned out, he was drafted, but not until 1942.

Running into my room, excitement bubbled up inside me as I attempted to open the V-mail. Government mail from overseas came on very thin paper after it was reprinted from a thumbnail-sized microfilm image. The saving of space and weight allowed successful delivery of tons of mail from overseas. Despite my attempts at delicacy, I ripped a section of my letter and had to tape it together before I could read it.

February 22, 1944

Dearest Lizzie,

I am still in England, but I can't give you any more information in case the enemy intercepts the letter. I can tell you this much: I miss you and hope this war will not keep us apart for too long.

The censors won't allow me to say anything about what I'm doing, or where I am, so the only thing I can comment on is the weather. It's awful! We have not seen the sun for five days, and today a storm with gale-force winds and pellets of rain roared down on us like bullets falling from the sky. It is unseasonably warm, so when it's not raining, the fog encompasses us with a white blanket and the only daylight I see is where I stand.

Enough about the weather. Let me tell you about the food. In polite conversation, I would call the army's favorite meal "chipped beef on toast," but since I am a soldier now, I call it by its real name: "shit on a shingle!" I've been told once the invasion starts, SOS. is the only food we'll get.

I'm sorry if I'm painting a bleak picture of army life, but I want you to know I am safe and think of you every day. Yesterday, in front of the Officers' quarters, I saw a Harley Davidson WLA motorcycle and thought of you assembling the engine. Maybe your fingerprints were on the crankshaft.

I don't know if it's possible, but I felt a connection, real or imagined, that you were with me. I miss you so terribly much.

Please write often, as I am lonely and far away. I carry with me the gold coin your father gave to you on our wedding day, and I feel you near me. Thank you for entrusting me with such a precious gift.

Your loving husband,
Fred

After reading the letter three times, I went back into the kitchen where my mother and father were getting ready for dinner. My parents, now in their sixties, worked together preparing our dinner of meat, potatoes, and green beans. Clarence was unlike most men of his day in that he always helped my mother with the household chores, and he was a fabulous cook. He grew up in an all-male household where he was responsible for meal preparation. Flossy, my mom, enjoyed the comforts of growing up with a successful father and didn't like doing any of the cooking and cleaning. Somehow, they made it work, and my brother and I grew up in a peaceful, loving home.

When Fred went overseas, I moved in with Dad and Mom and left my bookkeeping job at my dad's newspaper to work on the assembly line at Harley Davidson. My father understood my desire to support the war effort but didn't like the fact there was nobody left to manage the finances at his newspaper. Fred's sister, Ruth, followed my path and got a job at Harley. We were best friends and wanted to do whatever we could to make our country strong.

While Fred was overseas, I enjoyed moving into the former bedroom of the house I grew up in and spending time with my parents. They were generous, goodhearted people and happy their daughter was close while their son, my brother Carl, was in the air force overseas. Clarence and Flossy had owned the house for more than thirty years, ever since they were first married. They met at a rally for the Socialist Party in Milwaukee when Clarence was a member of the Carpenter's Union, and my mother was the daughter of the owner of the Socialist newspaper. After dating for a short time, they got married, and Clarence took a job at the newspaper. Eventually, he became a managing editor and ultimately bought the paper and grew it into the largest Socialist newspaper in the Midwest.

Clarence donated a lot of his time and money to the Socialist Party, but I never subscribed to his political ideology. Even though we disagreed politically, we were close, and he taught me accounting and the business of running the newspaper. That's where I met Fred, who worked as a printer.

"Did Fred have anything interesting to say?" Clarence asked as he checked the roast beef for tenderness.

"Just that he is safe and hates the food and the weather. And he misses me."

"That V-mail system is pretty effective," my dad said. "It cuts down on the weight of the mail and makes delivery more efficient. I should investigate the possibilities for the newspaper. Maybe this war will bring about some positive changes."

"Well, first you'd have to figure out a way to make the paper stronger and keep it from tearing. That would be useful," I added.

"When the war is over and you come back to work for me," my dad said, "you can be our efficiency expert and figure it out."

"Sure," I said. "I'm a bookkeeper, not a scientist."

"Hey, I'm a farmer but I figured out how to become a newspaper mogul."

We both laughed because that was actually true.

I watched my parents cook together and admired their teamwork. There was a flow to their movements coming from years of togetherness and understanding. Clarence was tall, lean, and striking, but his once youthful good looks had given way to an expanded waistline, thinning hair except for the bushy white eyebrows, stubbles growing everywhere on the lower half of his face, and creases etched across his forehead. Flossy, on the other hand, still had her youthful glow. Frequent trips to the beauty salon for expensive treatments, had slowed the ravages of time.

Everybody loved Clarence. He was sociable, outgoing, and when he spoke there was an infectious smile on his face and a twinkle in his blue eyes. But there was also something guarded about him, an internal unrest. He was an enigma to me, and I sensed the unrest below the surface of his gregarious personality. I would love to have known him in his earlier years.

One time when I was a young child, my parents had a family gathering at our house. Relatives I barely knew came to visit. I was intrigued by what they said about my dad's early life, so when my parents left the room, I hid in a corner behind the curtains and listened to my aunts talk about my dad and his brother.

"That was so tragic about Ernie. Clarence seems to have gotten over it," said Aunt Mathilda. "I loved those boys, but they were so different."

"I think twins have a special connection. They look alike but have their own personalities," Aunt Louisa added.

Hearing this from behind the stuffy curtain, I silently gasped. My hands covered my face, preventing me from inhaling the dust and sneezing. I did not want to give myself away because

I wanted to hear more. What special connection and what twin? I knew nothing of this.

Aunt Louisa continued, "I think when Clarence was left out of the will, it left an indelible mark on him. It's a good thing he met Flossy and found a career that suited him. He was so restless."

"It helps she agreed with his politics."

"Don't forget, his socialist views coincided with her father's newspaper. That ideology does not fit with our family." Aunt Louisa laughed.

"I know, but so be it!" said Aunt Mathilda. "We still love him."

Thinking back on that day, I remembered being totally confused by my aunt's conversation but never asked anyone about a twin. I'm now old enough to ask those questions and I want to know what happened.

After dinner that night, my dad sat alone in our living room, writing in his notebook. My mother was busy in the kitchen, so I went to the living room with the intention of solving the family mystery.

"Dad," I said. "What are you writing about in that journal? Is it a mystery?"

"I have written about many family mysteries in this diary, but right now I'm trying to create a new column for the paper. The title is, "Stories from the Front." I want people to stay in touch with local soldiers and keep morale high."

"Sounds like a good idea to me." Sinking into the soft leather chair next to my father's desk, I rubbed my hand over its buttery texture and felt comfortable. The rest of the living room looked like vintage Victorian. There was a couch that had been slept on too many times, chipped and broken knickknacks collecting dust, a picture of Carl and me in a plastic swimming pool with Clarence and Flossy proudly looking on. This room was filled with memories of a childhood filled with sunshine and love. I wanted that with Fred.

I began, "When I was a little girl, I once overheard Aunt Mathilda and Aunt Louisa talking about you when you were still living in Brandon. I was hiding in a corner of the living room behind the drapes, so they didn't know I was there."

"Naughty girl," my father said with a grin. "What did you hear that you should not have?"

"They talked about the farm, and I remember you told me about your great experiment to set up a cooperative farming system. You said the other farmers didn't buy into it and refused to take part."

"That is true." My dad's gaze shifted to the kitchen where my mother was working. Readjusting his posture, he sat upright and called for my mother to come and join us.

"I can't right now," she replied. "I have work to do."

Glad that my mother was giving us this time alone, I pressed, "Tell me what happened."

"You already know. I eventually sold the farm to Uncle Augie. He loved it and built it into a big operation."

"Yes, I know," I continued, "But I don't know anything about your life there."

"That's because I had no life until I moved to Milwaukee and met your mother. She changed everything. Then you and Carl were born, and I had it all!"

My father tried to relax into the curvature of his favorite old chair and reached for his glasses and newspaper, effectively ending our conversation.

"Who is Ernie?" I blurted out.

Something flashed in my father's eyes, but only for an instant. I couldn't recognize the emotion before it disappeared. "How do you know about him?"

"I heard Aunt Mathilda and Aunt Louisa talk about him. They said he was your twin. I didn't even know you had a brother, not to mention a twin."

Removing his glasses, he hesitated before saying, "Yes, I had a twin named Ernie, but he died a long time ago."

"How come I never knew about him? When did he die?"

"It was a difficult time in my life." My father's face washed blank; his muscles frozen. He ignored my question and tried to go back to his paper.

"Just tell me what happened," I pleaded. "Now that I see your reluctance to talk, I want to know more."

"It's hard for me to talk about," my father said, looking for comfort in the familiar surroundings of our living room. He inhaled deeply and started cautiously, measuring each word so as not to give too much away. He began, "When I was a young punk, I hated living on the farm and hated the physical work it required. I had big dreams of moving to the city. My dad did not approve, and we argued a lot about work, about my social life, and about my then girlfriend. One day, I just up and left and moved to Milwaukee. Our relationship deteriorated to the point where we rarely spoke."

"Is that when you met Mom? You said she changed your life."

"I wish I would have met her then. Everything might have been different. What happened was that Ernie moved home after school, and he and my father worked together on the farm. Apparently, they formed a bond that I was not a part of, so when my father died unexpectedly in a farming accident, I discovered he changed the title on the farm deed a few days before the accident. Ernie inherited everything."

"That's not fair," I said, jumping to my feet. "You should

have gotten your share of your father's property. I bet you were mad."

"I was," my dad paused a moment, a twitch surfacing in the corner of his eyes. "This is the part of my past I'm ashamed of. I hope you're able to understand."

"Of course I am," I said, shaking my head in disbelief.

"I never wanted the farm," my father continued. "But once I knew I could not have it, it suddenly became my obsession. All I could think of was how to get what I felt was my inheritance."

"Dad," I said, "that's not so unusual. I always want what I can't have."

"True enough," he proceeded, "but I was not content to let it go. I sued my brother for half of the farm but lost."

"What?" I said, "I can't believe you sued your brother!"

He saw the shock register on my face before I could hide it. Looking away, he said, "When I found out Ernie got the farm, I wanted to hurt him, so I went to our house and found Dad's gold coin, the one I gave you on your wedding day. I took it, knowing it had sentimental value for Ernie. That was my way of getting back."

Confusion clouded my mind. I couldn't believe my father would do this. After a moment, my thoughts cleared enough to remember the coin. "I gave that coin to Fred when he was shipped overseas. I put it in his hand on our last night and wished him luck." My hands started to shake as my mind spun out of control. "Are you telling me the coin could bring disaster instead of luck?"

My father looked troubled as he shifted his gaze to the kitchen where my mother was still working. He sighed and said, "It has not been lucky for me, but I hoped it would bring you joy."

"I gave it to Fred to guide him safely home. I'm superstitious about these things and now I'm worried."

"Don't be worried." My father continued trying to reassure me. "It may have brought me luck by getting me to Milwaukee, but for sure, it never harmed me. Fred will be fine."

"I know," I settled back into the chair. "There is more to your story than the taking of a coin. How did you end up with the farm?"

"That is the worst part." My father composed himself, quietly looking at me before he continued. "I don't talk about it because it is the low point of my life. According to my family and those who knew Ernie, he never recovered from the ordeal of the lawsuit and the stress of losing both his father and his brother. He fell one night, hit his head, and died. I inherited the farm."

"What? You mean, just like that he fell and died? That doesn't sound right." I turned in my chair so I could face my father head on. "You mean you inherited the farm from Ernie?"

My father nodded slowly. "Ernie's death devastated me. People said Ernie changed, and I think he would still be alive if I hadn't caused so many problems."

"You don't know that," I said.

"Yes, I do. Ernie didn't just fall and die, and he didn't drink and lose his balance. He changed because he couldn't handle the stress of his loss. People around him said he would disappear, sometimes for days, and not remember where he had been. My uncle thought he had amnesia and advised him to see a doctor, but he insisted nothing was wrong."

Tears welled up in my eyes and I proceeded cautiously, the words not coming easily. "Have you been carrying around this guilt your whole life? Why did you keep it a secret from me, from everyone?"

"I didn't want you or Carl to know how selfish and stupid I was. The harm I inflicted was immeasurable. I thought knowing about it might diminish me in your eyes." My dad paused, fighting for control. "If it weren't for your mother, I would not be the person I am today. I owe her my life."

"We all owe Mom our lives," I said.

I got up from the chair to hug my father. He stood also, and we hugged with a power that pulled us together but still allowed us to breathe within our own space. "I am proud of you," I said, gaining some composure. "After all that, you went on and had a good life. You gave both Carl and me a wonderful childhood."

"Maybe," my dad said with little enthusiasm. "But the past is still there."

March 14, 1944

Dearest Lizzie,

Hiya, you might notice I'm adding some British slang to my letters, as we have spent time talking to locals in the small city where we're stationed (sorry, I can't tell you where). The weather is bloody awful, and I fancy an evening at home with you by my side.

Enough of the British stuff, but I do want you by my side.

I think I can tell you this without the censors blocking it out. I'm in the munitions unit, and I'll work behind the front lines once the invasion begins. This is a safer place than in the infantry, where my brother is, or—like your brother— dropping bombs over Germany. So don't worry about my safety. I'm fine.

I've become friendly with another soldier in my unit who

is learning how to weld. He says he plans on starting his own business in Cincinnati once the war is over. His name is Al, and when I told him about you, he said we have an open invitation to visit him once this war is over. Do you think you would like to visit Cincinnati?

Life is very tedious here. And did I mention lonely? I think about you all the time and can't wait until I can get home and can hold you in my arms.

Your loving husband,
Fred

Whenever my loneliness became unbearable, I resorted to my favorite pastime: reading. When I received Fred's letter, I was in the middle of reading *A Tree Grows in Brooklyn* by Betty Smith. I chose that book because the army produced a mass-market version to fit in a uniform pocket. I fantasized that Fred and I were reading the same book at the same time, and our thoughts synchronized. We were like the tree, growing together and becoming stronger no matter what obstacles stood in our way.

"You are such a dreamer," my mother said as I ate breakfast and told her about the book. "Don't you realize you are seven time zones away? You will never be reading at the same time. It's time for you to go to work. Get going or you'll be late."

The Harley-Davidson plant where I worked was on the west side of Milwaukee. My father drove me downtown in his Studebaker Champion, and then I took the streetcar the rest of the way.

When I got to work, my friend Ruth was already at her station on the assembly line.

"Anything new?" I asked.

Ruth tilted her head so her red curls fell to one side. "Nothing new," she said. "All I know is George is somewhere in England, preparing for the big invasion. He hates the weather!"

"Same here," I responded. "Last night I reread letters from Fred and listened to *The Firestone Hour*. They had the original music from *Babes in Toyland*, and I like 'March of the Toys'."

"Sounds exciting," Ruth added sarcastically. "Don't we have a basketball game tonight?"

"Yes, we do," I said. "I'll meet you at the gym at six p.m. We can warm up because we play the Bombers, and they have that girl with a dead-on shot. She is impossible to defend."

"How can you say that?" Ruth gave me a vicious look. "I am an ace defender. If anyone can shut her down, I can."

"I hope so. You realize this game could be a preview of the championship?"

"Will we have leather balls tonight?" Ruth complained. "The last time we played, the balls were flat, and the rubber felt like plastic. Just because the Japanese control the rubber in Malaysia doesn't mean we should go without good basketballs."

"I don't think the Japanese will ruin our basketball game. Everybody plays with the same ball." I snickered.

Our league played six-on-six Iowa Girls Basketball rules and had three forwards and three defenders. The forwards did the shooting and stayed on their half of the court. Defenders were on the other half and were not allowed to cross the centerline. Players could only dribble twice, and then had to shoot or pass. Those rules seemed silly to me, and I never could understand why we had to use them while the boys could run the full court and have a lot more fun.

Despite our best effort, we lost to the Bombers but still made it into the finals because we beat everyone else. At the finals, we met the Bombers again. "Tonight's the night. I'm pumped!" I said to Ruth, entering the gym with a swagger of confidence that I only partially felt.

"Do you really think we have a shot at it?" she asked.

"Of course we do. I'm a great forward and you can handle any defense that comes at you. We'll be unstoppable!"

Ruth laughed at my confidence as we got ready for the City Conference Women's Basketball Championship. Basketball was one of the few sports available to women during the war years. It was good exercise and, according to men, didn't put a strain on our nervous systems. This, of course, was rubbish, as our nervous systems could handle any situation as well as any man's. We just wanted to have fun, and we thrived on the competition and camaraderie.

Once in the gym, we watched the men's team practice on the far end of the court. Their championship game followed ours.

"Will you just look at those guys over there?" I said as we gawked at them like starry-eyed schoolgirls.

"They're so tall," Ruth said. "I couldn't get close to blocking one of their shots even if I had a pair of those All-Star Converse sneakers."

"I think they can touch the basketball rim if they jump high enough. I don't think Fred could do that, and he is tall, but not like those guys."

"Those guys are not eligible for military service because of their height," Ruth added. "They're staying home and getting all the good jobs. Wait till our husbands come home and take their jobs away from them."

We started the game with enthusiasm on our side and the determination to eke out an upset, but by halftime we were down five points. "I need some water," I yelled as I approached the bench. I sucked in a lungful of air and gulped an entire bottle.

"Ruth, your face is on fire."

"I know," said Ruth. "And my whole body is shaking. I've never been so exhausted and we're only at the half."

"Look at the Bombers," I said, looking at the opposite side of the court. "They look fresh. What's wrong with them?"

"I want to be on their team!" Ruth said as she splashed water on her crimson face.

"No, you don't," I countered. "I think they train harder than we do. We have other things on our minds. It's supposed to be fun, not a life goal."

Early in the second half, a serious foul almost took me out of the game and sent me flying to the floor. A Bomber defender tried to tie up the ball outside of the lane and knocked me over with her power. According to the rules, that was an illegal move, and the referee called the foul. The defender thought I was intimidated because I was slow to get up. She was wrong. I was shaken, but it only served to infuriate and motivate me more. After the incident, I scored three baskets in a row.

Unfortunately, the Bombers outlasted us by a score of 48 to 44, and our exhausted team walked away with a consolation prize: a cheap plastic medal in the shape of a basketball. We were upset about the loss, but not upset enough to cancel our gathering at Turner Hall and drown our sorrows with a cool glass of beer.

"Hello to the victorious basketball team! Have a cold one on me!" shouted Michael, my cousin on leave from the Navy. Others greeted us with cheers even though we lost the game. By the looks of Michael's glassy eyes and his unsteady stance, I knew he had been there a long time. It was good we didn't go into overtime. Michael was on a two-week leave after having spent the past seven months in the Mediterranean on an attack cargo ship.

"Thanks," I said, "but you got the wrong team. We just couldn't get past the Bombers, and we're not here to celebrate but to drown our sorrows."

"I can't believe anybody could defeat you gals. You're maniacs out there," Michael replied, signaling to the bartender for more drinks.

"We played as hard as we could," Ruth said. "What a letdown! I wanted that championship so bad."

"Well," said Michael, "I'm only here for another two days, so we need to celebrate *something*. What should it be?"

"Anything except basketball," I said.

"I've got something to celebrate," Michael said with enthusiasm. "I was in the Mediterranean for close to seven months and never saw any fighting. My timing was perfect. When I went overseas in October '43, the fighting in North Africa was over and the July invasion of Sicily was complete. No fighting for me! I missed the September invasion of Italy, so once again, I dodged a bullet. Let's celebrate my war effort!"

Michael walked over to the jukebox, put in some coins, selected a Bing Crosby tune, and started to canvas the room for eligible girls. With a gleam in his eyes, he danced with every single one of us, making us laugh and forget about the world for a night.

———————— ◆ ————————

May 30, 1944

Dearest Lizzie,

I am still in England but getting bored and restless. The

army doesn't tell us anything about our mission, but we are constantly moving around in what seems like endless circles. I think the army's motto is: Hurry up and wait. We know an invasion is coming, but we don't know when or where. It's a security issue—the same reason I can't tell you anything about where I am.

I don't mean to sound so dreary, but it is hard to wait. To pass the time, my friend Al and I often talk about our wives, and we laugh at the cute little mannerisms both of you have. The two of you are actually very similar, and I think you would enjoy meeting them. You could talk about us and compare notes.

I don't know how long these letters take to get to you, but you will probably hear about the invasion before I can get another letter out. The army shows us newsreels about American soldiers fighting in Italy, and they look happy and successful, but to me it seems dangerous. I want no part of that fighting. I can only hope our troops will end this war soon so I can get back to you.

Love,
Fred

The morning of June 6, 1944 was like no other, and I will never forget every detail or emotion of the day. It began with the usual brush teeth, wash face, have breakfast, but at seven a.m., our local radio station announced, "Supreme Headquarters, Allied Expeditionary Forces has just announced the invasion has begun! Repeat, D-Day has come."

Everyone knew it was coming, but knowing it was happening now left me uneasy. Fred's letters said he operated in the background, behind the lines, but was that true? Maybe he told me that so I wouldn't worry. Maybe the Army decided at the last minute to put him on the front lines. I tried to stay calm, but anxiety bubbled inside me and filled me with fear.

When I walked into the kitchen, my mom took one look at me and knew what I was going through. "Lizzie," she said, "I heard the news on the radio. You shouldn't worry about Fred. You know most of the soldiers on the front line are the young kids that can handle the physical demands. Fred is thirty and I'm nervous just looking at you."

"I know," I said, "but Fred is still going to have to cross the channel at some point. He needs to get to those beaches safely."

"He won't cross this early in the invasion," my mom said, her arms wrapped around me in a tight squeeze. "Breaching the shoreline comes first and that will take a while."

"I suppose," I responded, thankful for her comfort. "If only we could communicate, I would feel better. The only thing the censors let through is talk about the weather and the food. I feel so alone."

"We're all in the dark," said my mother. "We just have to stay strong."

My dad came downstairs, looking as somber as I felt. "Do you need a ride to work? I don't know if the streetcars will be running today."

"No," I said. "The Harley factory closed for the day and wants their workers to pray for a speedy end to the war."

Outside I could hear sirens and distant factory whistles calling us to prayer. Businesses closed and most factories shut down. Bells rang across the country, including the Liberty Bell, which had not been rung since 1835. Nobody wanted to do anything except listen for news.

Later in the morning, I switched from our local news to CBS

World News, hoping to get more current information. Allied broadcasts were not forthcoming, and the only information getting through came primarily from German media outlets. Those sources reported the invasion was on, but news of any successes or failures were not being reported.

At three in the afternoon, President Roosevelt came on the radio to soothe the American public:

Many people have urged that I call the nation into a single day of special prayer. But because the road is long and the desire is great, I ask that our people devote themselves in a continuance of prayer. As we rise to each new day, and again when each day is spent, let words of prayer be on our lips, invoking Thy help to our efforts.

After a sleepless night, I went back to work determined to do my part in our war effort. Almost all the women on the assembly line had husbands, brothers, or sons overseas, so each of us worked with nervous energy, increasing the productivity of the assembly lines. It would be impossible to keep up that pace, but for now, assembling motorcycle parts felt like our mission.

After work, I caught the streetcar downtown to rendezvous with my dad. On the way home, we were silent, each with our own thoughts, until I asked, "Do you think I'd know, deep inside of me, if something happened to Fred? Do you believe his spirit would come to me?"

My father was pensive for a moment before he said, "I believe you and Fred are emotionally connected, and you would have a feeling if that bond became broken. Right now, what you have is fear, but that makes you human. It also makes you brave."

"I don't feel very brave," I said.

"Remember our talk about Ernie," my dad unexpectedly said. "The connection I have to him is still there, even though he is physically gone. The guilt I had regarding his death changed me into a better person because his spirit is still with me. Fred is with you."

"I want to believe I'll know if his spirit comes to me," I said. "I'm just not sure. I'm looking for certainty where there is none."

"Lizzie, you need to put your worries aside. Think of the benefit you add to the war effort with your job. That should give you some certainty and a sense of value."

"Fred believes I'm adding value," I said. "He told me he's not on the front lines, so I'll focus on his value behind the scenes."

"Good idea," my dad said.

Once home, I listened to the news on the radio. They were reporting the Allies were successful in taking the beaches but sustained heavy causalities. No numbers or any other information was available.

That night at dinner, my father tried to distract me from my worries by talking about his plan to help the war effort. "I'm going to print more human-interest stories in the paper," he said. "Keeping morale high is important, and I can help by giving my readers firsthand accounts of soldiers living overseas. I cancelled a lot of advertising, so there's room for special stories to connect families. I think people need that and I want to help."

I was too lost in my own thoughts to comment on my father's, so he added, "Maybe the newspaper should send a reporter overseas to interview local Milwaukee boys to see how they are faring."

I remained silent until it was obvious that I didn't feel like talking. Realizing this, my dad changed the subject.

"Remember when I took you to the 1940 mayoral convention? We sat in the audience when they nominated Carl Ziegler for mayor. His party released a room full of balloons from the ceiling to announce his candidacy."

"I remember. It was crazy. But what does that have to do with the war, or with Fred?"

"Maybe nothing," my dad said, laughing. "But it made him popular. My candidate, Dan Hoan, a great socialist mayor, couldn't measure up to the show Ziegler put on even though he was the better candidate."

"I know, Dad, but that still has nothing to do with the war."

"Well, maybe the balloons don't relate to the war, but they do show the power of entertainment, and I wanted to lighten your mood and remember we can still laugh."

"I'll try to remember."

Yet another letter came from Fred, just in time to assuage my anxiety.

July 25, 1944

Dearest Lizzie,

I want to come home. It is horrible over here. I can tell you where I've been but not where I am now, so here is the latest.

My unit was not part of the D-Day invasion but was held back at Cherbourg. Cherbourg is a city on the Normandy coast that has a naturally deep harbor, and the allies needed it to bring in supplies, so that's what I'm doing now.

In mid-June, a huge storm wiped out the artificial harbors built on D-Day. Our troops were running low on supplies and ammunition. The army couldn't get resupplied because ships couldn't get into the shallow harbor at Normandy. The deep harbor at Cherbourg had to be opened.

The invasion at Cherbourg began on June 25 with days of bombardments and fighting. My unit shipped out across the channel transporting supplies to the battered troops. Entering the harbor was treacherous because of underwater mines and other booby traps left behind by the German army. Once safely anchored, I couldn't believe what I saw. The entire town was demolished, rubble strewn everywhere. A few buildings still stood, and some local people walked around looking for food and supplies, but it was a mess. Tanks grinding and roaring up and down the streets crushed anything in their way making sure the town was secure.

Also, the local French people have not been friendly; they do not see us as liberators. Just the opposite, they resent our presence and the damage our bombs did to their town. They don't care if they pay taxes to Germany or France; they just want to be left alone. The sooner I get out of France, the happier I'll be.

We get some reports about the activities of other divisions, but I don't know exactly where my brother Jim is, or my cousin Warren. They're both in the infantry, so I assume they're in France, maybe even close to me, but we're not told anything. Is your brother Carl still based in England?

Let me know any news from home. You know how much I miss you.

Your loving husband,
Fred

Fred and I corresponded frequently, but the mail was erratic, and when I didn't get a letter for a few days, I became worried and depressed. Fred assured me he was not in harm's way, but reading between the lines, this endless war disheartened his spirit and he was tired of it. He never said he was miserable, but a wife has a sense about these things.

I needed to do something to get out of my doldrums because I was emotionally drained. My friends at work were supportive, and many of them were in the same situation, but we never engaged in lighthearted, fun conversations. Only work talk and war talk. Plus, the assembly line was getting boring.

I talked to Ruth after work one day. "Do you want to go to a movie this weekend? *To Have and Have Not* is playing at the theater downtown."

"I'll go," Ruth said with enthusiasm. "Doesn't it star Humphrey Bogart and Lauren Bacall?"

"I think so," I responded. "I've heard it's a wonderful movie with sizzling love scenes. Bogie and Bacall married after the movie, so the on-screen romance is more than just good acting!"

"That's all we need," Ruth added "Sizzling love scenes to get us all excited before we go home to our empty beds."

"Ruth, let's just go and have fun. We both need a break."

We went to the movie that night, but before the show, the theater ran a newsreel about our armed forces. There were clips showing military training, women in the work force, war bond drives, and some actual footage of soldiers in Italy moving homeless civilians away from their shattered homes into places outside of the fighting zones. They referred to it as one of the great rescue achievements of the war.

"Are our husbands involved in this?" I asked Ruth after the newsreel finished.

"Absolutely not." I heard anger in Ruth's voice. "Our husbands are also homeless and sleeping outdoors but expected to survive as well as fight the Germans."

"Are you sure?"

Fred had never told me anything about feeling homeless or having difficult living conditions. All he'd ever told me was that he was safe.

"I think these newsreels are propaganda meant to make us feel good so we'll be patriotic and support the war. I'm not sure they have a lot of validity," Ruth said.

"You are always so pessimistic. Look at how happy our troops made those Italians. They were grateful to be rescued."

Ruth gave me a sideways glance. "I think the Army puts a positive slant on all the news. They need to keep us supporting them."

A few weeks later, another letter from Fred arrived.

August 15, 1944

Dear Lizzie,

I don't have time to write a long letter because we are very active now that the war is progressing. I am still safe and not in harm's way, but I worry about the other family members fighting over here. I suppose no news is good news.

I am in great health and I hope the same is true for you. I don't love the food but am used to it and don't complain. I'm part of a team that takes care of munitions and other supplies, but I have no idea where the supplies go once they leave our camp. We hear rumors constantly, the latest one being that our troops are on their way to Paris, but nothing is confirmed.

Our officers are always optimistic and say we are winning the war, but they do not divulge any details.

I hope I will be home soon.

Love,
Fred

With so many of my family members fighting in the war, it was only a matter of time before we got the dreaded Western Union telegram starting, "I regret to inform you . . ." On August 10th, Fred's brother, Jim, was wounded fighting in France, and he died ten days later.

An army officer and a Western Union courier delivered the telegram to Jim's mother. It said Jim's body would be temporarily buried in a military cemetery in France. When the war was over, the body could return home for a proper burial or be buried in a national cemetery in the United States or Europe at the Army's expense. Ruth called me from her family's home on Montana Street, where everyone had gathered to mourn the passing of Jim. Jim's mother tried being brave, but the Façade of quiet coping was gone, and she was inconsolable.

I quickly changed my clothes and left for their house. Fred, Ruth, and Jim grew up in a typical one-and-a-half story Milwaukee bungalow. The half story consisted of an A-framed attic with a finished bedroom in the front, above the porch. The porch was large and welcoming, and once you stepped inside, the hardwood floors and beautifully crafted wood cabinets made you feel at home.

In happier times, children would play in the small front yard, but today, the sadness of a family tragedy surrounded the porch and dirtied the air. Jim's fiancé sat on a swing at the far end of the porch, trying to stifle sobs and hide the rawness of her grief. Salty tears streamed down her face as her body trembled under the weight of her emotions. Friends tried to comfort her, but nothing could close the open wound only time would heal.

I glanced to my left and saw a service flag hanging in the

window. The white flag with the red border originally had two blue stars in the center, indicating there were two family members serving in the armed forces. Now there was one blue star and one gold star.

Seeing the gold star sent me into shock, and I tried to breathe deeply but my body was too tense. I felt empty. The gold star signified that Jim was gone, but I feared the remaining blue star would change to gold and my husband would disappear.

"Lizzie." I heard my name but did not respond. "Come inside," Ruth said, trying to bring me back into focus.

I tore my eyes away from the flag. "I'll be right there," I said. "Give me a minute." I wasn't yet ready to face Fred's family.

When I finally walked into the house, I could feel the grief encircling the room. Nobody was talking, many were crying, and others just stared into space. The gathering included family, neighbors, school friends of Jim, and a few military personnel. Most of the women were in the kitchen cooking, trying to do something familiar or comforting, but nobody was hungry and most of the food went to waste.

Ruth walked right up to me and gave me a hug. Her eyes, which usually sparkled, were swollen and dark. Her curly red hair was unruly and tied up in a messy ponytail.

"I'm so glad you're here. My mother is a mess. I've been trying to get information from army headquarters, but they don't know anything, or so they tell me."

"Where was Jim stationed?" I asked. "Was he in France, anywhere near Fred? How about George? Is he safe?"

I rattled on with questions even though I knew Ruth had no answers. I couldn't stop myself and knew I was losing control. My hands and legs started to tingle and go numb. Ruth made me sit down and rest for a minute.

"All we know," Ruth said in a forced calm tone, "is that Jim was shot and taken to an army hospital but did not survive his wounds. He died ten days after being injured."

I wasn't satisfied with the explanation and panicked. "When Jim wrote home, did he ever tell you he was in any danger?" I paused only to take a breath and continued with a barrage of questions. "Did you know if he was on the front lines? I need to know where Fred is and what he's doing. He could be in a hospital or lying in a ditch."

"Slow down," Ruth said. "Jim never talked about the war in any of his letters. Maybe his fiancé knows more, but I don't want to ask her now."

In the weeks that followed, I had difficulty concentrating on anything. My job got more boring by the day, family life turned into a series of polite conversations, and even letters from Fred were sporadic and mundane. I was lost in a permanent state of inaction. When Ruth came up to me after work one day and told me her cousin Warren died somewhere in France, I could not respond. The final blow in this trilogy of tragedy came when my brother, Carl, died in a training exercise over England, shot down by friendly fire. All the crewmen perished. I cried for weeks.

When a letter from Fred finally arrived, I was relieved to know he was safe.

October 21, 1944

Dear Lizzie,

I am still fine and missing you. We heard reports that our Army chased the Germans out of Paris, and it seems as if we are winning the war. At least our officers are optimistic. I hope to bring you a souvenir from Paris, even though I don't want to go there and can't wait to get home.

The news about Jim and Warren shattered me, and I'm having a hard time adjusting. An officer notified me they were stationed only three miles from where I am, but I didn't know. No details were given about Jim, but Warren was killed when twenty German tanks met his group of infantrymen who were spearheading an attack.

My unit does what it can to keep doing our job. Al and I rely on each other to keep our morale up, so we look for things to lighten our day. We don't find a lot, so most of the time we just talk about home and what we're going to do when the war ends.

How are my mother and sister dealing with this stuff? I never thought this war would go on for so long. The strength and training of the German soldiers is amazing, and now I understand why our ancestors had such a strong work ethic. It's in their blood to work hard. It seems weird to fight people who could be our distant relatives. I don't want to think about it.

I miss you.

Love,
Fred

Time moved slowly. Winter set in and Christmas passed without my husband being home. I continued to get letters from Fred saying he missed me, but each letter got shorter. I was tired of hearing about the weather and irritated with his lack of significant information. I knew the death of his brother and cousin affected him, but I was also losing my patience as an emotional distance grew between us.

One evening, Ruth and I met for a few beers after work.

"What's new with Fred?" Ruth asked as she sipped a

Braumeister, a new beer from the Independent Milwaukee Brewing Company.

"Fred seems fine," I said, "although he doesn't give me a lot of information. By the way, what are you drinking? The guy on the label looks like Santa Claus without a beard."

"I think he actually is Santa Claus, because he brings me good cheer." Ruth downed her beer like a child who hasn't seen water for a week. "I wonder if our husbands get good Milwaukee beer overseas," she mused. "I'm sure German beers are not on the Army's list of preferred beverages. When the guys get home, they're going to be hungry for good beer, as well as a few other things."

I giggled, enjoying my private thoughts. "I think we should plan a fun event this weekend to get our minds off our problems. Do you have any ideas?"

We looked blankly at each other until Ruth finally said, "This is an odd situation. We all have enough money for fun, but between rationing and our husbands overseas, there is nothing to spend the money on."

I agreed. "Last summer, we couldn't even get cream puffs at the State Fair due to rationing. I hope the war is over by next August so we can taste our favorite desserts!"

"I heard there's a bond rally at Schuster's department store on North Third Street this weekend," said Ruth. "Ben Barkin is speaking. He's head of the local war finance committee.

"Let's go. At least I'll have something to look forward to besides another boring letter from Fred."

It took me a few seconds to realize what I just said. I called Fred boring, which he was not. In truth, I missed his sense of humor.

"Did I just hear you accuse Fred of being boring? You're

calling my brother boring?" Ruth's laugh sprung out of her like a leak, slow at first but ramping up into a crescendo. "You're married to the guy, and you just realized that now?"

"What are you talking about, Ruth? Fred is funny and he makes me laugh. He would be so upset if he knew I was complaining about him. I feel bad I said that."

"Lizzy." Ruth finally controlled her laughter. "Fred has a lot of good qualities, but sense of humor isn't one of them. Don't feel bad for saying something that is true. We all have some give and take in our relationships."

"I know. I just can't deal with this war thing anymore."

That weekend, Ruth and I went to Schuster's for the bond rally. In the middle of Ben Barkin's speech on the value of war bonds, I turned to Ruth and whispered, "I heard about these bonds the last time I listened to *Fibber McGee and Molly* on the radio. You buy one for $18.25 and after ten years it's worth $25. Plus, it helps the war effort."

"Sounds like a good deal to me," said Ruth. "But I'm more interested in who those three soldiers are standing just behind Ben Barkin."

"I was wondering the same thing. They look like kids playing soldier, except one of them lost his leg."

"Ben Barkin really knows how to work a crowd. Anyone here would lose their heart to those baby-faced Irish grins."

"How do you know they're Irish?" I asked.

Ruth rolled her eyes at me. "Just look at the sign next to them. It says, 'Meet the Three Mulqueen Brothers.' That's an Irish name if I ever heard one."

"Unfortunately," I said, "a grin can't cover up a lost leg.

C'mon, let's go buy some war bonds. We'll feel like we're doing something."

After purchasing the bonds, we decided we needed something more. It was early spring, and the long cold winter was behind us. No more snow and harsh winds, but warmer days ahead. We hopped on a streetcar and went downtown. I hoped that being near people, walking along the river, absorbing the vibrant sounds of the city, would quiet the restlessness inside me.

We got off the streetcar across from the Pabst Building and walked toward the river. Standing along the walkway, we watched the water traffic slowly pass by, a few pleasure boats, but mostly barges heading into the city to deliver goods. I thought of Fred crossing the English Channel and wondered if the channel water was as cold as the water coming in from Lake Michigan, or maybe colder.

Ruth interrupted my reverie. "Look at all the people over there by the bridge. I wonder what they are doing."

"It's probably Gertie the duck," I said, turning my gaze away from the water and toward the growing crowd of people. "They run a daily series in the newspaper about her. My dad even picked up the story for his paper."

"Let's go see." Ruth was already ahead of me as she rushed for the duck.

Once there, we worked our way through the crowd, gently elbowing those in front of us until we reached the edge of the bridge where we saw Gertie sitting on her nest. She had built the nest on top of wood pilings, laid her eggs, and was now protecting them. Despite throngs of visitors and motorists, noises, and distractions, Gertie was able to screen out the turmoil and protect her family.

"Oh, look," someone from the crowd said. "Gertie is sitting on her eggs."

Another person responded, "I don't see the father anywhere. Maybe he's fighting a duck war someplace else. I bet she's lonely."

"Not as lonely as me." My sadness drained through me. This duck, this symbol of perseverance, survived to protect her family. I must do the same and not let my sadness consume me. I had to find a way to cope.

My unhappiness eased after my next letter from Fred. He sounded happy, as if the war might really end.

April 25, 1945

My Dearest Lizzie,

I think the war is almost over, because we hear rumors of the Germans retreating and our troops advancing. My company is moving from Antwerp toward Paris, passing through bombed-out cities and a landscape that shows the impact of tactical bombings. You cannot believe what this war has done to this country.

Since we won the Battle of the Bulge back in January, I can say a little more about my location because the censors are not as strict. You may have guessed I was in Belgium. It was cold and gloomy, and I would have killed for a dry, warm pair of socks. The weather is starting to warm up now, but all I can think about is coming home to see the flowering trees in our backyard and breathe the fresh Lake Michigan air.

The army is full of rumors, and there are talks of horrible camps run by the Germans where people were treated inhumanely and slaughtered. We have not seen any of these camps, but I have seen starving people on the streets in ragged

clothes, looking so thin I wonder how they can walk. We give
them chocolate bars and they act as if we have saved them from
the gates of hell—maybe we have.

How are things in Milwaukee? Jim is constantly on my
mind, and I worry about my mother. I can't wait to get back
home to see you.

Your loving husband,
Fred

Spring brought new hope to our war-weary city. The
flowering crab trees in our backyard were in full bloom, and the
bulbs we'd planted the previous fall sprung out of the frozen
soil into dazzling flowers in an array of colors. The sad, dreary
winter was behind us.

Living at home while Fred was overseas had its benefits
because we were one of the few households with a useable
telephone. Western Electric had halted its production of
telephones in 1942 due to the retooling of factories for military
equipment, but my parents already had their phone by that
time.

One Saturday morning, I called Ruth.

"Do you want go shopping today?" I asked. "We could go
down by Mitchell Street."

"You betcha!" she said. "The war news is good, and I want
to buy a new dress for when George comes home. Let's meet at
Schuster's where the streetcar bends the corner round."

"Great," I said. "I'll meet you there at eleven."

Schuster's was a fantastic department store because they
carried the latest chic styles in woman's clothing. A new dress
would cheer me up and prepare me for my long-awaited
reunion with Fred. I wanted the newest design, something with

padded shoulders and a skirt coming down to my knees. A belted waist would be nice to emphasize my hourglass figure. If I had any money left, a hat and gloves would complement the perfect outfit. Shoes and a new purse were probably out of the question.

I sorted through the racks, looking for a dress that matched the image in my mind's eye. I ended up buying a patriotic blue and white print dress which emphasized my curves. I'd add a red scarf to complete the ensemble.

"Lizzie, that dress is gorgeous on you," Ruth said. "I like the red, white, and blue theme you're going with." She moved to the far end of the department and desperately flipped through several more racks of dresses, getting discouraged with not finding anything she considered suitable.

"I need to stop eating before I invest in a new dress," Ruth said. "Do you think I can lose five pounds by the end of the day?"

I laughed because Ruth was always so self-deprecating. She was my sister-in-law but also my best friend, and she kept me laughing, which was hard to do with everything going on around us.

After rummaging through several more racks and forgetting her pledge to stop eating, Ruth declared, "I'm hungry. Let's go around the corner to the Goldman's lunch counter."

Goldman's was another department store but much different from Schuster's. The original building's exterior was red brick and strongly Victorian, but that façade was replaced by boring, washed-out green cement blocks. The building lacked style. The Victorian details were preserved on the inside with high ceilings wrapped with mosaics, dental crown molding, chandeliers, and wrought-iron rails. It was packed with oddities, relics, and mismatched odds and ends. Scattered randomly throughout the store, some right in the middle of the sales floor, were radiators. When walking on the Mezzanine level, you had to be careful not to bump your head on the heating ducts hanging at forehead height. The food counter could be found at the back of the store. Round, green-cushioned stools allowed people to sit and enjoy lunch, or have the special of the day, an open-faced pork cutlet with mashed potatoes and gravy. It looked good, but after buying a slenderizing dress, I thought better of ordering the special.

We sat down to enjoy our lunch when I noticed two strange-looking men at the counter across from us. Dressed in worn-out clothing and looking unwashed, they were out of place in this commercial store. I overheard some of their conversation.

"Wo Kann ich gutes Milwaukee-Bier finden?"

They were obviously speaking German. I only recognized two words, *Milwaukee* and *bier*, but it wasn't hard to figure out they wanted to find a place to get beer. They were probably hoping to find someone who spoke German, and although Mitchell Street was primarily a Polish neighborhood, there were plenty of people who would understand their native tongue. *"Verkaufen sie Bier?"*

"Nein," said Ruth, who knew a little German from her grandparents. *"Was machst du hier? Sie sind nicht aus Milwaukee?"* she angrily yelled at them.

The men quietly got up from their stools and moved toward the door, but as they turned around, two uniformed army officers walked up to them and said, "Halt." The officers turned to us and asked, "Are these men bothering you?"

"No," I responded. "Who are they?"

"They're German prisoners of war escaped from Camp Billy Mitchell, where they're being detained. They were captured in North Africa and shipped over here because the army couldn't afford to keep them overseas."

We gasped, shocked to find out we had POWs in Milwaukee.

"Our husbands are fighting the Germans in Europe, putting their lives in danger, and these guys are in our homeland drinking beer? What is going on?" Ruth exclaimed.

"These guys didn't escape to make war," one of the officers said. "They're just looking for beer."

We found that only mildly amusing. "Don't worry that you're in any danger because there are no Nazi Party members at Billy Mitchell. Just conscripts, ordinary Joes," the other officer explained.

"That doesn't matter," I countered. "They don't belong here, eating our food and drinking our beer. They should be punished for the things they are doing to American soldiers."

The officers nodded to us as they secured the prisoners with handcuffs. "Don't worry, they work in some of our farming fields and in factories making batteries. Nothing military. In fact, we're getting ready to close the camp and ship these guys over to England or France and let those countries deal with them."

"Good riddance," said Ruth.

———————◆———————

May 15, 1945

Dear Lizzie,

It's over! You probably already know, but I wanted you to hear it from me, so you believed it. I spent close to a year in Europe under horrible conditions and now all I want is to come home. The end is in sight.

We heard stories of bells ringing and dancing in the streets of Paris, but for me, it was the same kind of day I have had for the last several months. When the announcement came

*through that we were not to fire at the Germans anymore,
I didn't believe it and wanted assurance it was over. The
Germans fought hard right to the bitter end.*

*A peculiar thing happened a few days after V-E Day. We
saw a German officer enter our camp on a motorcycle sidecar
(not a Harley!) and ask to speak to the commander in charge.
In broken English, we overheard him saying he wanted to join
the American Army and fight the Russians. Our commander
told him the war was over and there would be no more fighting.
He grunted, left the tent, got back onto his motorcycle, and
drove away. No one stopped him or seemed concerned, and he
disappeared down the road. I don't know if he ever found any
Russians to fight.*

*I am making a list of things I want to do and food I want
to eat once I get home—it's a long list! We'll probably stay in
Europe for a while, as there is a lot of cleanup to do and many
displaced people to help, but all I can think of is getting back to
you and our life together.*

Love,
Fred

After the war ended, I quit my job at Harley-Davidson and
went back to work at my dad's newspaper. Being a bookkeeper
was far more rewarding than drilling bore holes on an assembly
line. I moved out of my father's house and into the house on
Montana Street Fred had recently inherited from his mother
after she passed.

The night before Fred returned, I spent hours in the bathroom preparing for our reunion. I wanted a Lana Turner look:
soft, flowing curls gently pulled away from my face, forming
a victory roll along my forehead. After several attempts with

hairspray and bobby pins, I decided it wasn't working for me. I wasn't Lana Turner, and I don't know how those hairdos ever stayed in place. I decided to go with a deep side part, flat top, and fluffy neck curls. This was more like me.

When I reached the train station the next day, it was already packed with eager wives, friends, and families. A band was playing patriotic songs, and as the train pulled into the station, the crowds erupted with *hurrah!*

I saw Fred before he saw me. He was leaning out of an open window, looking around and waving. I felt my heart leap; he looked so thin and tired, and all I wanted to do was hold him, comfort him, and never let go. I fought my way through the mass of excited people, keeping my eyes focused on his face. When he saw me, he smiled, and I melted.

I ran up to the window and Fred leaned out to kiss me, but we were too far apart, and the train was still slowly moving. I pushed and shoved my way to the exit platform, and once he descended the stairs, I ran into his arms and collapsed, crying and shaking at the same time. We moved to the outside of the crowd and found a small corner where we could properly greet each other.

"I never want this moment to end," I said between sobs.

Fred looked at me with tenderness. "You can't imagine how much I missed you. Every day, I held you in my thoughts, and that got me through the tough times."

"We only have a short time before we have to leave for your Welcome Home party, so let's make the most of this time alone." We kissed until I stopped crying. His arms folded around me and I melted into his body. I felt like I was dreaming.

"Don't ever go away again," I choked out.

"Don't worry. I'm all yours."

After a two-week vacation, Fred went back to his job at the newspaper and I thought we would settle into our pre-war existence, but things were different.

"How was work today?" I asked Fred one night.

"Okay," he said.

"I was working in the front office today, but I never saw you at the printing presses."

"I was there."

"Did any of the other guys help you set up the presses?"

"Nope."

I gave up trying to talk about work and tried a new approach. "Do you still want to go to Cincinnati sometime to see your friend Al? I'd love to meet him."

"Maybe," was all Fred said.

"I thought you wanted to see him and meet his wife."

"I do, but we can talk later."

I held back on any discussion of the war, but I was getting frustrated by Fred's lack of communication. "I talked to Virginia today," I said. "You know her. She married my brother Carl, and they have a baby. She is still living in Brandon and has no place to go since Carl died."

Fred's eyes suddenly glazed over and his expression turned into a frozen mask. He looked at me with vacant eyes but didn't say a word.

"I may go and visit her next week," I said. "Do you want to come along?"

Fred walked away, not saying a word and leaving me to wonder what I said or did to upset him.

Later that night, as we sat together listening to music on the radio, Fred's hands began to fidget and his knees bobbed up and down. When he spoke, which was unusual, he didn't make eye contact but instead stared at something (or nothing) in the far corner of the room. Finally, I asked, "Is there anything you want to talk about?"

"Not really," Fred responded. "I just need time to get used to being at home. You should listen to this music without me. I'm going to bed."

Fred left, leaving me in a state of confusion.

Several months passed and an emotional wedge inserted itself between us. Communication became awkward and we only discussed trivial matters like the weather (just like in his letters). I gave up asking him about the war because those questions angered him and, ultimately, he withdrew. The fun-loving guy I had married was now distant and short-tempered.

One afternoon, I took a break from work and walked the short distance to Gimbel's department store to enjoy the Christmas decorations. My spirits lifted as I neared the intersection and saw the red and green streamers framing the large storefront windows. As I got closer, the creative work of a window designer depicted a scene of a happy family celebrating together and exchanging gifts. The dioramas showed people looking joyous, loving, and perfect. I lingered for a while, thinking of the contrast between those scenes and my life. Would I ever find happiness again? The war changed everything, and my husband no longer made me feel wanted.

Ruth and I still got together at Turner's on Thursdays after our basketball games. We needed time, not only for basketball, but also for camaraderie and girl-talk. "Great game tonight. Excellent defense, Ruth."

"You were great, too," Ruth said. "You scored twelve points!"

"I had the weaker defender on me, so I could get open to

take the shot," I said. "I also had so much pent-up energy; I was able to run circles around the other team. I guess anxiety made me a better player."

We ordered some beers and started to talk. "Can I ask you a question?" I began. "Fred has not been the same since he got back from the war. I'm worried about him. Do you notice a change in George, or in Fred?"

"Not in George, except for his plans for our future. He wants to move to Chicago, where his family has political connections. He's been talking about that for a long time. Fred, on the other hand, I can see is totally changed."

"What kind of change do you see? With me, he is so distant."

"Are you kidding me? He is not only distant, but his anger is unpredictable. My brother has always been temperamental, but he got mad at George last week for ordering the special at White Castle instead of a burger."

I realized Fred's problems were more obvious than I thought, and they were not just directed at me. I took a deep breath and continued. "Fred doesn't look at me when we talk and he's always nervous and fidgeting. One night at dinner, I was trying to make light conversation and told him a story about a disagreement I'd had with a co-worker. He told me to stop feeling sorry for myself and not be so selfish. He said I didn't know what bad was and stormed out of the room. We didn't speak for three days. I don't know what to do anymore because nothing I say pleases him."

Ruth was silent for a minute, but finally spoke up. "Lizzie, you are such a people pleaser, and definitely not selfish. My brother has always been a little moody, but this is ridiculous."

"It's good to hear," I said, feeling better. "I've been doubting myself and feeling insecure."

Ruth understood my concerns. "I've heard it's common for

this kind of thing to affect soldiers when they come home from war," she said. "They're irritable and have nightmares and a lot of other stuff. They call it 'battle fatigue'. That sounds like what Fred is going through."

"Maybe, but what can I do about it? I want my old Fred back. He didn't even fight on the front lines, so he shouldn't be suffering from fear or fatigue."

"You never know," said Ruth. "I knew someone who ended up in therapy because he came home from the war and couldn't function on his job."

"Fred would never go to therapy," I said. "He thinks that would mean he's crazy. His philosophy is 'act normal and you'll feel normal.' Unfortunately, he is neither acting nor feeling normal and he won't talk about it."

"This is not a quick fix," Ruth said.

As the weeks passed, Fred seemed to become more and more withdrawn. He insisted on sleeping with a light on because he said it made him safe. He was always nervous and easily startled by noises. He never complained about feeling sick, but his eating habits changed, and he got angry if I added seasoning to his food or prepared a new meal. Once a hearty eater, he was now picky and ate only to sustain himself.

To complicate matters, I thought I was pregnant. I knew I had to tell Fred, but I was afraid of his reaction. Since coming home from the war, he seemed to have a need to protect me, despite his angry outburst directed at me. He was impossible to figure out, and the added responsibility of a baby could overwhelm him. How would he treat a new baby? And was it fair to bring an infant into a family this dysfunctional? I had to do something.

The next day, after work, I stopped at the local butcher

shop and bought a top-loin roast beef for dinner. Next stop was the corner grocery store for potatoes, vegetables, and a pie for dessert. I thought mashed potatoes, gravy, and roast beef followed by cherry pie would put Fred in a good mood.

I was working in the kitchen when he got home. "What's for dinner?" he asked.

"I'm making a special treat for you tonight. Why don't you wash up while I get this ready?"

I set the table and lit some candles, hoping a romantic atmosphere and good food would ease us into a relaxed but meaningful conversation. My pregnancy should be happy, joyful news, but I had butterflies in my stomach.

We sat down to dinner. Fred didn't notice any of the extra effort I went through, but at least he said, "This roast beef is delicious. It's been a long time since I've had such good food."

The anxiety I felt earlier eased and a new optimism recharged my spirit. I smiled at him as my brain whispered, "This is going to work." Fred looked content, as if taking a break from his worries. The semblance of a smile appeared on his face, making me think that he was enjoying the evening.

Feeling bold, I started the conversation. "I got the best cut of beef for dinner tonight, so we can enjoy ourselves and think about what we want to do this weekend."

"I don't have any plans for the weekend," Fred replied as he put a spoonful of mashed potatoes in his mouth. I continued eating, thinking about how to bring up the subject of the baby, but when I looked at him, a sudden bolt of panic shot through me. Fred's features transformed, and I saw a different man across the table. His clear blue eyes were now clouded spheres fixed at a spot in the corner of the room. His lips became narrow, craggy lines of anger, and his chin jutted forward, creating a caricature of the handsome face I'd fallen in love with.

"What's wrong with these mashed potatoes?" he bellowed. "Did you put something in them? Did you add garlic? You know I can't eat garlic!"

"I didn't know you couldn't eat garlic, and no, I didn't put any garlic in them."

Fred was now in a full-on rage.

"I do everything I can to protect you, and still you're trying to make my life miserable. I can't eat this. At least get me some coffee so I can feel alive."

My usual passivity evaporated in the face of Fred's anger. I matched his fury with my own, feeling a volcano of resentment bubbling up inside of me, ready to overflow.

"I've had enough tiptoeing around your moods and being blamed for things beyond my control. Why can't you figure out a way to love me? We never talk, we never go anywhere together, we never enjoy each other, and we rarely make love. It's a good thing we did a while ago because at least I'll have a baby who loves me."

"A baby?" Fred glared at me.

"Yes," I said defiantly.

"When were you going to tell me? Was I supposed to discover it on my own?"

"You were supposed to know, to understand, to sense, or, at the very least, *feel* something. If you ever paid attention to me, you'd see the changes, but you are oblivious to anything except your own misery."

Fred was speechless. When we'd argued in the past, I would placate him until he calmed down, but I was sick of it, and I was sick of him.

"You are not alone." Fred's voice became mild, but the tension etched into his face remained. "I need to get some sleep. Leave me alone for a while."

I was shaking with anger as Fred turned away from me and walked into our bedroom, slamming the door.

I took a deep breath, trying to calm my nerves. I busied myself cleaning up the kitchen and lamented the waste of a good loin roast. I turned on the radio; the *Amos 'n' Andy* show was airing. I hoped the hardworking Amos and the shiftless Andy would make me laugh and distract me from my problems, but it was hard to shift my focus to something as trivial as a comedy.

After cleaning up the kitchen and turning off the radio, I forced myself to go into the bedroom to see if Fred was asleep. The room was dingy with the stale smell of sweat, and I felt unwelcome. Fred was thrashing from side to side in our bed, mumbling indecipherable words as if he was in the middle of a horrible nightmare. My earlier anger forgotten, I saw only the shell of the person I had fallen in love with, and I ached for the man he once was.

I shook Fred until he woke up, frozen in panic. His eyes flew around the room as his fingers clenched into tight fists, ready to strike. He did not notice I was there but turned toward the wall and fell into a deep sleep, the nightmare over. In the morning, I asked him about his dream, but he refused to talk. I wanted to talk about therapy, but I knew that would only cause another explosion, and with the pregnancy, I didn't have the strength to fight him.

Over the next several months, as our baby grew inside me, Fred seemed to soften, and his unpredictable anger lessened. He became interested in my pregnancy and enjoyed going to checkups with me. Fred and the obstetrician would talk together about the baby's growth and development, but would leave me out of the discussion, as if I had nothing to do with this child.

"I think everything will be fine with Lizzie's birth," Dr. Schmidt said on one visit. "We will probably put her in a twilight sleep with some drugs, but I don't think we'll need a scopolamine cocktail."

"What about me?" I asked, barging into their conversation. "Don't you want to tell me what you're going to do to my body?"

"Don't worry," the doctor said. "You won't feel any pain. Some mothers believe in natural childbirth, but it hurts quite a bit. This is a better approach."

"Just make it safe and fast," said Fred. "Can I be in the room for the delivery?"

"No, it's not allowed, but you will be the first one to find out the baby's sex," Dr. Schmidt said, trying to appease Fred.

On the way home, Fred and I discussed the delivery. "I'm afraid of the pain," I said as Fred swerved to the middle of the road to avoid a squirrel.

Looking out of the rearview mirror to see if he hit the squirrel, Fred said, "Don't worry, the doctor is going to give you something so you won't feel a thing. He said it would be safe and fast. Better than the fate of that squirrel," he added with an attempt at humor.

"I'm glad you think so. You're not the one carrying this load inside of you. And I don't care about that squirrel."

"I know, Lizzie, but I have faith in you."

"You just say that so I'll stop complaining. This is no small thing, and you are so distant and secretive. I want your support. I don't want you telling me what you think I want to hear."

"That's not what I'm doing."

"That's what it feels like."

My pregnancy was uneventful, and as the delivery date approached, I felt more and more inclined to talk to Fred about the lingering issues between us. Although Fred eagerly awaited the birth of the baby, we still did not communicate openly or share the emotional bond we'd once had. I did not want to bring a baby into this house of silence.

One more time I tried my old trick of cooking a romantic dinner to get Fred to relax and talk to me, only this time I made sure to substitute broccoli for the mashed potatoes. "Are we going to take the baby to Cincinnati to see Al once he or she is old enough to travel?" I asked.

"Maybe," Fred answered. "Do you really want to meet them? They just had a baby, and with Al starting his own business, they're busy."

"I'd like to meet them and hear about your time together in England and France. You never talk about it and maybe Al can give me a few more details."

Fred did not initially respond, and I thought he was going to shut me out just like he always did, but the opposite happened. His face softened and his words began to flow, like a broken dam that suddenly opened its floodgates. Thoughts and memories that had been deeply buried came to the surface, and Fred began to share his story.

"As you know, my company crossed the channel into Cherbourg a couple of weeks after D-Day. We were not told the number of causalities suffered in Normandy but only that we were victorious and advancing into France.

"Once on land, my company set up a base for maintenance of the artillery and delivering supplies. As the war progressed, we moved further west, following the path of the frontline troops. We would set up camp and resupply, then move and set up another camp, resupply, and move again.

"Then the full impact of the war hit me. I was notified that Jim was wounded while fighting and taken to an army hospital. I tried to get a pass to visit, but my commander would not allow it. Ten days later, another message came, this one informing me of the death of my brother. My friend Al was of great comfort to me, but I could not get over my feelings of guilt and regret for not having done something.

"I no longer felt safe. The pain I had wasn't in my body, it was in my heart. All I could think about was survival. My actions centered on staying out of harm's way. I was selfish in my actions and not a good soldier.

"In November, we headed toward Antwerp. We didn't have time to set up tented camps, so we slept in abandoned foxholes, bunkers, or abandoned barns. Starving peasants greeted us wherever we went and begged for food or chocolate. Young children hung out of the windows of ruined houses, looking to us for protection, but all I could think about was how to protect myself.

"My feet were killing me. I think I wrote you about wanting socks more than food, and you probably thought I was crazy, but you can't imagine how sore, cold, wet feet can affect you. I would crawl into my mummy bag at night, hunched against a barn wall, or nestled between two rocks, and talk to my feet, urging them to move better and do their job. They didn't.

"I thought about you every minute of every day. In an abandoned house, I found a set of dishes and knew you would love the china pattern. We were not allowed to take any souvenirs, so I snuck out one night and buried the dishes in a spot I was sure I'd remember. I marked it with a pile of stones in case I ever returned, so I could dig them up and bring them home to you. Now I think of how foolish that was because I will never go back to that ravaged country again.

"After the end of the war, we headed toward Paris. The longer we were on the road, the more depressed and withdrawn I became. The remnants of war littered the landscape and skeletal people, or an occasional German soldier, lay dead along the roadside. I would see Jim's face in each dying soldier, his smiling expressions frozen onto a corpse that would never return home.

"When I saw you at the train station, I felt a rush of emotions and was lost in the happiness of our reunion. I wanted to cry with relief but was afraid you would think me weak and foolish, so I just held you tight.

"I know I have not been a good husband, but I am trying to get us back to the free, easy love we used to have. I want to be a good father and bring this baby into a peaceful, safe world with two loving parents, but I need help. I need you to understand why I am sometimes distant, and I promise I will try to deal with my problems and to love you."

I wiped the tears from my eyes and embraced Fred. We hugged for a long time and I felt the warmth of a connection. This was the new beginning I was hoping for.

We finally let go. Fred and I made eye contact, the first in a long time. A quiet calmness grew between us, like a salve soothing our broken marriage. It took me a while to compose myself, but I slowly looked into Fred's teary eyes and asked, "How did you know what china pattern I liked?"

Both of us started to laugh, an uncontrollable release of tension. Fred reached into his pocket and pulled out the gold coin I had entrusted to him when he went overseas.

"This has kept me safe from danger and brought me home

to you. I give it back to you now for safekeeping and good fortune. One day you will pass it on to our children."

———————

I delivered my baby in September, a little girl we named Kim. Everything about her was special and she filled a place in our hearts we never knew was empty.

When we brought Kim home from the hospital, I prepared lunch while Fred took her into the living room, sat down in a rocking chair, and turned up the volume on the radio.

"What are you doing?" I asked, checking to see if Kim was startled by the noise.

"I want her to get used to noise so she'll be able to sleep uninterrupted by sound."

I took a deep breath and watched the two of them, my husband and my daughter, peacefully rocking together. I knew we were starting a journey that would have many bumps along the way, but hopefully, it would be a journey that would lead us to peace.

KIM

ROUND FOUR

MARCH 29, 2009

There is something unsettling about the faint aroma of jasmine. I noticed it when I started chemotherapy, but now it's taking me back to a time my memory has difficulty accessing. I was able to disappear for a while into the wartime letters between my parents, but they only reminded me of the distance between me and everyone I love. I was right. We are cursed. And it ends with me and my son. The worst part is that he had to go before me.

I'm in the hospital for my fourth round of chemotherapy, but my mind is in another place, a place with grief so thick I can't break through its web-like strength. It is barely visible, like the silk of the cobweb, but it surrounds me, circles my being, and holds me in a place where I only see Billy. I cannot return to a life where jasmine is healing, a soothing lotion I put on my baby's hand to lull him to sleep.

Billy moved to New York after law school and was an associate at a law firm in midtown Manhattan. Because the cost of living was so outrageous in the city, he found an apartment across the river in Bushwick. Back in the seventies, the Bonanno crime family controlled Bushwick and was the scene of some major mafia hits. Today, like so many other Brooklyn neighborhoods, the area has been gentrified and is an edgy, hip place to live with imaginative street artists and eclectic coffee shops.

When Billy first moved to Bushwick, Mark and I were afraid

that it was a dangerous place, an area of crime and leftover mafia families that would not be safe for a young lawyer. Billy assured us we were wrong and invited us to see his apartment.

We rendezvoused in midtown for an early dinner and then took the Number 3 Train to Brooklyn where we got off at Clark Street. Billy explained this was not his usual stop, but he wanted us to walk on the Brooklyn Promenade at dusk to enjoy the view of the New York skyline. It was dazzling. With the setting sun creating a backdrop for the massive buildings of steel and glass, the city twinkled like a million eyes inviting you into its sphere. I understood why Billy wanted to become a part of it.

We left the Promenade and walked several miles to Bushwick, meandering through the many neighborhoods of Brooklyn, soaking in the smells of ethnic cooking and the chatter of multiple languages. By the time we reached Bushwick, we were exhausted by the exercise but exhilarated by a beautiful night spent with our son.

Billy's apartment was on the seventh floor of a ten-story pre-war building. Mature green ash trees formed a canopy over the street and provided a small piece of nature in this otherwise concrete jungle. Pollution and exhaust fumes penetrated the crevices of the building's dull-red bricks, making the structure look old and worn. A few window boxes tried to brighten the exterior, but flowers do not do well without sunshine or clean air. I steadied myself to think positively because this was not the kind of place I envisioned for my son.

Billy lived in a small studio apartment. He said it accommodated his lifestyle and gave him easy access to midtown Manhattan via the subway. The apartment was unremarkable, one big cube with a combined living and sleeping space, a bathroom, and a kitchenette. I thought back to my first apart-ment in Chicago, which was not much bigger but accommo-dated two people, and how horrified my father was the first time he visited. "What kind of place is this?" he looked around with disgust. I was not going to do that to Billy.

I did notice a few things Billy added to create some coziness in this barren space. He put curtains on the windows so the tenants in the next building could not see in, he tried to brighten the interior by adding more lights, and on the windowsill he placed family photos. There were pictures of Mark and me hugging on our twentieth wedding anniversary, the three of us skiing in Colorado, and another bodysurfing on sunlit waves in South Carolina. Those were happy times for all of us.

Mark and Billy took a seat on his cushy secondhand couch and talked about business. I sat across from them on one of the two kitchen chairs, not participating in their conversation but observing the love between father and son. I was so proud of Billy that I did not notice the restlessness in his body, the distracted look in his eyes, the tightening of his fists, the vulnerability that would have been obvious had I not been seeing him through a mother's eyes.

Looking back on that time, I ignored every sign of a problem. The stress Billy was feeling should have been obvious. Worried behaviors like fidgeting and agitation were visible but ignored by me. Billy masked his feelings behind a façade of happiness, and I should have seen through it. All indications of a problem were there, but I was oblivious. I am a psychologist, and I should have known, but I did nothing. I wanted the comfort of being with my only child, loving him and letting his presence wash over me. Now he is gone.

The first three rounds of my treatment are over and there are three more to go. The drugs are fighting my diseased cells internally, but externally, I'm losing the fight with myself. Selfishly, I think about death—who will come to my funeral, who will cry, and who will remember me a year from now. Family and friends will mourn and say nice things, but they don't understand. This cancer, for me, is a way out of a grief I can no longer live with.

Mark doesn't understand the depth of my grief. We started our marriage right, both of us taking emotional risks and giving ourselves into each other, but since Billy's death, our marriage has disintegrated. We have different ways to cope, different ways to grieve, but the result is an unsatisfying love that hurts both of us. It's like we're standing on distant shores. We see one another, and we send letters, but it's hopeless. I don't have the hope that Lizzie had. Maybe I used to. My heart breaks for Mark because he will be left alone, but he has the strength to make the right choices and repair his life. I'm the one who wants the easy way out.

Since my last treatment, a new problem has raised its ugly head. The fog is getting easier, but my forearm is red and swollen just below the needle's insertion point. Dr. Belmont takes a long, serious look at the wound, touching and poking the surrounding areas. Returning to his chair, he hesitates a moment before explaining that the swelling and redness is due to some of the chemo drugs leaking out of my veins.

"How bad is that?" I ask, thinking my vein is now a sieve.

"It could be dangerous because it causes a chemical burn, which, if it happens repeatedly, may result in permanent damage to your tissue. I think the IV is no longer viable. We'll have to try something else."

"What does 'something else' mean?"

"We'll have to go with an alternative to the IV. We can insert a PICC line."

"And what's that?"

"It is a form of intravenous access used for longer periods of time. It's painless and I promise it will make everything easier."

"Go ahead," I say, not even looking at him. I don't question his decision or ask for more information. It's just one more obstacle to overcome.

Once I'm in The Chair, Mark leaves to do errands. I reach into my tote bag to retrieve my family album and Clarence's diary. I left my mother's letters at home because they are too fragile to carry around. After all of the studying, reading, researching, of diaries, newspapers, and photographs, I still have not found any medical information connecting a family member to Lymphoma. The Lymphoma came from somewhere other than my DNA.

I feel surprisingly calm coming to this conclusion. Initially, I was so sure there was a genetic reason for Lymphoma, but what I found in my family history, was not a medical connection but rather a character, a personality, a physical resemblance that traveled through generations and ended with me. Each generation that preceded me had their own battles to fight, their own medical obstacles to overcome, but they were strong and found a way. They all had the legacy of the gold coin to guide them, and even though it did not always bring luck, it did bring strength. I am a part of that legacy.

Mark comes back from his errands and asks me how much longer the chemo will take. I tell him I don't know.

"I was thinking of Billy," I say, feeling a need to share my hurt. "When I first looked at these pictures, I was trying to understand my family. Instead, everything reminds me of Billy and what we lost."

Mark looks away from me and I can almost see a shell closing around him. "Billy's death will always be a tragedy, but it is not part of your illness."

"I know that. Billy did not cause my cancer; how could you even think that?" Rage fills me.

"I didn't mean to imply Billy caused your cancer. It's possible the stress of losing Billy created tension that could affect your health. You understand what stress does to the body."

"I do." This is the first time in a long time Mark and I even mentioned Billy's name. I can see tension in his eyes and across his forehead. He can't make eye contact.

I drift off and say to no one in particular, "At this point, it doesn't matter what caused my cancer. I don't plan on coming out of it." I gasp and inhale deeply as I realize what I just said. I had no intention of expressing those thoughts, especially to Mark.

Mark turns away from the window and looks directly into my eyes. He moves closer, invading my space. "What are you saying? You are a strong fighter."

"Maybe I was once." I pause to catch my breath. "But I don't have the energy anymore."

"You cannot really be thinking that way. The treatment is working."

"It doesn't matter. We are in trouble and have not connected on an emotional level since Billy died. It's hard, I'm miserable, and I'm not sure I want to survive this cancer."

Mark is overcome and cannot speak. He withdraws and doesn't even try to weave himself back into the conversation.

"I'm sorry," I say. "I didn't mean to lay this on you. You know I will continue with the treatment and make the most of the time I have remaining, but I can't live with this sorrow any longer. I feel an unforgiving weight on me, and I cannot get out from under it. Cancer has given me the way out."

Mark and I turn away from each other, both of us looking outside at the rising and falling waves of Lake Michigan. The sunlight is creating diamonds on its surface, but we are not aware of its beauty. Our thoughts are choreographed in different directions. We will never be in sync.

"No." Mark is crying. "Cancer will never be the way out."

I turn away from him. I turn away from the future. I've looked all I can into my family's past, and I don't see anything in my own future. I don't see Billy. I grip the coin, remembering how it came into my hands. With everything I've ever faced, the coin is the one thing I've never lost. Even when I was lost.

CHICAGO
DEMOCRATIC NATIONAL CONVENTION

KIM
AUGUST 1968

S arah was adamant. "Kim, you have to go to the Festival of Life. It's organized by Jerry Rubin, Abbie Hoffman, and Tom Hayden as a counterbalance to the Democratic National Convention. They call it the Convention of Death."

"What do they call the Convention of Death, the DNC or the Festival?" I asked sarcastically.

"It's just a metaphor. Interpret it as you like," Sarah said.

Sarah was my best friend from college, my confidant, and now my roommate in Chicago. We met at the University of Wisconsin where both of us were students, Sarah in education and I in psychology. Sarah was an activist, a member of the Students for a Democratic Society, and involved in sit-ins and anti-war protests on campus. I was just a hippie who liked the slogan "Make Love, Not War."

"I don't want to go to Lincoln Park for any festival," I said. "There will be enough demonstrating in the next four days to make our voices heard."

"No," Sarah pleaded, "we have to begin with a celebration to get us ready for the action that will follow."

We did end up going to the Festival of Life, but it fizzled

out because Mayor Daley would not grant a permit for a music and entertainment festival. There were others at the park disappointed by the demise of the festival, and they were trying to get a rally going by shouting slogans into a loudspeaker. Nobody was paying attention to them because they were totally disorganized and just wanted to get in front of a crowd and rant.

"Let's make our own fun," urged Sarah.

"We're going to have to," I responded. "Let's get out of here."

We found a secluded area of the park, away from the demonstrators, and lit up a joint to "get a better perspective on life." The sweet smell of marijuana drifted in the breeze, and others soon joined us. We did not need the Festival of Life because we had a particular kind of party, filled with drug-infused humor and political bantering. At eleven p.m., the police announced the park was closing, and I got up to leave.

"Where are you going?" one of our newfound friends asked.

"I'm getting out of here because I don't want my head bashed in by those police over there," I stated. "There's going to be trouble and I'm too wasted to fight back."

"I'm staying a little longer," said Sarah. "I'll see you back at the apartment."

"Okay, see you there," I said and left.

By that time, I had enough of politics and partying. I never learned the names of any of the people with us, but they were from all parts of the country who came to Chicago to exercise their right to demonstrate. I admired their passion, but tonight I was drunk, stoned, and tired. I just wanted to go home.

The park was dark, but muted tones of black, green, and brown created the feeling of an underworld habitat. A line of policemen stood at attention on the edge of the park wearing helmets and holding clubs as if they meant to attack like knights charging into a village. The reflectors on their uniforms created patterns of light that assaulted me, and I sensed the power they emitted. I hurried past them as fast as I could into the brighter street, but those lights seemed whiter and brighter than usual. I needed to get home.

Stumbling along the way, I managed to avoid any contact with the police or anyone else. I made it to our apartment, rummaged through my purse for the keys, opened the door, went straight to my bed, and fell asleep. The next thing I remembered was yellow rays of sunshine sneaking through the cracks of my window shade.

"Oh, my aching head. It feels like a toothache in my brain. Where are some cold tea bags and cucumber slices?"

Reluctantly pulling the soft sheet from my face, I opened my eyes and the memory of an evening of fun and foolishness flowed into my consciousness. "What was I thinking going to Lincoln Park last night?" I rubbed my bloodshot eyes and willed my saliva glands to go into overdrive so I could swallow and remember what I'd done. Where was Sarah? Did she make it home last night?

My headache was fierce as I got out of bed to find an aspirin. Sprawled on our secondhand couch, Sarah was passed out, arms splayed and legs hanging over the side. This was not the first time we'd been in a situation like this, having been at the University of Wisconsin in the '60s. We had ample opportunities for anti-war demonstrations and the parties that followed. Being in Chicago at the time of the DNC was the perfect opportunity for us to become active on a national level.

Walking past Sarah to put on a pot of tea, I looked at our small apartment and felt lucky to have found something in the cool neighborhood of Lincoln Park. The apartment was vintage, but not the charming kind with old-world craftsman-ship and cozy niches. Ours was dingy, with no natural light, and claustrophobic. It was the antithesis of a magazine cover, with no color, no dining table, no bookshelves, no accent pieces, and no ambiance of any kind. It was a room waiting for a new personality, but neither Sarah nor I had the means or the time to fix it. That didn't matter to me. I was on my own and I loved it.

My politics supported the anti-war movement since it began, but until eight months ago, I was a passive participant. Then Sarah talked me into joining her at a sit-in to protest on-campus recruiting by Dow Chemical, and everything changed.

"We're doing a 'sit-in,' right?" I asked Sarah at the time. "Nothing in front of a camera where my dad might see me?"

"Yeah, it's at the Commerce Building."

"I'll go with you, but I'm not sure I want to get involved," I said.

Hundreds of students crowded into the Commerce Building, filling every corridor with wall-to-wall people and making movement nearly impossible. Sarah and I forced our way into the Dean's office while the Dean busied himself trying to get the students out.

"We're not leaving until the university agrees not to allow Dow to recruit on this campus!" shouted one of the students.

The Dean remained calm and said, "If people want to work for Dow Chemical, they should have the opportunity to interview."

From the back of the room someone else shouted, "The United States is dropping napalm on children in Vietnam, and Dow Chemical is making it possible!"

"If you don't clear this room immediately," continued the

Dean, "I will have to call the police and have you physically removed."

Another protestor countered with, "It is our duty to prevent wrong from happening, and this is wrong."

The shouting within the small space escalated and emotional fervor erupted. Nobody could move, and we could barely breathe because the atmosphere was so toxic. Sarah's passion brought me into her orbit of increasing zeal and made it impossible for me to back away.

"Kim, you need to get active in this movement!" she bellowed. "There may be violence, but we don't have a choice. We have to make them see how wrong they are."

"I'm with you, Sarah," I responded. "I feel powerful just sitting here."

I began shouting along with the crowd, getting more and more vocal.

"Sarah," I said above the noise of the crowd. "Look behind you, the police are at the door."

"Oh shit." Sarah scanned the room for an escape route. "There is a back door. Let's go."

Once the other students saw the police entering the office, they tried to scatter but there were too many and no room for escape. Beatings were taking place near the entrance and police handcuffed anyone who refused to move. Chaos ensued, and Sarah and I crawled under tables and around chairs to get to the back door, only to find it barricaded.

"How do we get out of here?" My panic rose as my passion rapidly turned into terror. I looked at the police with their helmets, batons, and plastic face shields, and I hated them; they symbolized tyranny.

"Follow me," said Sarah. "We're going out the window."

We were not the only ones looking for an escape. Everyone

was migrating to the side of the office where the windows provided an exit to the outside. We inched our way around the Dean's desk, which he had abandoned, and pushed ahead toward the open window. Reaching it, I looked down, realized it was only a six-foot drop, and didn't care. I leaped.

Hitting the ground and rolling on my side, I looked for Sarah. She landed just behind me. "Are you alright?" I asked.

"I think so." Sarah looked exuberant. "My heart is racing and given the number of drugs I've inhaled over the years, I have never been so high."

"That kind of high I can do without." It was frightening.

Sarah and I followed other jumpers to the front of the building, past a parking lot where a student was letting air out of the tires of the police vans. When a police officer approached him, he quickly ran away and melted into the hundreds of other students surrounding the building. What started as an act of civil disobedience turned into a mob of people shouting and forcing a confrontation.

I saw one group of protesters chanting *Sieg Heil!* and giving the Nazi salute to the police. That caused the police to use increased force, and I saw a student being driven to the ground and beaten. My stomach revolted, sending chills to every extremity of my body because I hated violence. At the same time, using the Nazi salute to make their point was not only bad judgement but completely wrong. My father was a World War II veteran, and probably many of the police officers were as well.

When we reached the front of the Commerce Building, we could see police charging into the door. Without warning, they fired teargas canisters into the mob, and one of those canisters ricocheted off a post and rolled past me. It was my first taste of tear gas, and it was painful. I couldn't breathe. My throat went into spasms of coughing, and my eyes burned and watered.

Recovering my equilibrium, I yelled at the nearest policeman. "What the hell are you doing?" I had another coughing spasm and doubled over, falling to the ground.

"Get out of the way!" the police officer shouted at me.

"I'm not in the way; I can't move," I said, rebuking him.

"You kids don't know when you've got it good. If you attempt to go into the building, you'll be arrested."

"You are totally out of line. Go inside and see how much you enjoy getting tear gas in your face."

A shroud of tear gas enveloped the students. The police were treating the protesters as criminals, beating some and injuring many. The scene inflamed me, and my anger erupted. I shouted at a student standing next to me, "This brutality is uncalled for. Our civil rights are being violated."

He looked at me and said, "Sometimes violence is the only way to make a point. The police are making their point now, but just wait. We'll be back."

"Do you mean violence is an answer?" I asked.

"Many times, it is the only answer," said the student. As he left, an envelope dropped out of his pocket. Running after him to return the envelope, I saw it was addressed to Karl Armstrong.

The rioting went on for hours. My emotions fluctuated between power and submission, exhilaration and terror, passion and fear. The protests continued for several days but I was done with it, for now. The unnecessary police response to the students became the catalyst that changed my thinking and brought me into the rebellion.

The blaring ring of the phone was so loud my headache returned with a vengeance. "Hello," I said, gently cradling the phone to my ear.

"Hi Kim, it's Aunt Ruth. How are enjoying Chicago?"

"I'm actually looking for a job right now," I said, having regained some of my mental functions after the previous night's party. "Turns out nobody is looking for an entry-level psychologist."

"Somebody will recognize your potential and offer you the job of your dreams. If not, you can come and work for me at the restaurant."

"Great, four years of college to become a waitress!" I quickly realized how ungrateful I sounded. "Sorry, I do appreciate the offer but I'm trying to find something in my field."

"I know," said Aunt Ruth. "That's not why I'm calling, anyway. Did you go to the festival in Lincoln Park last night?"

My aunt knew I was active in the anti-war movement, and she possibly had similar convictions, but she would disapprove of any action that could put me in danger. She walked a fine line between letting me be on my own and protecting me. When my mother died five years earlier, it was Aunt Ruth who vowed to watch over me and guide me through life. She was a second mother and tended to worry about me the same way a parent worries about the well-being of their child. She probably never thought I would turn into a revolutionary.

I couldn't lie to my aunt, so I said, "I did go to Lincoln Park, but I did not take part in any demonstrations."

"Good," she said. "George told me this morning there were beatings and arrests last night because the demonstrators refused to leave the park at closing. I'm glad you weren't there."

"So am I," I said, thinking I'd left just in time.

"The real reason I'm calling," said my aunt, "is I'd like to invite you to dinner at the restaurant. Your dad and his lady friend, Alma, are driving in from Milwaukee and I thought we'd have a nice family dinner."

"You mean 'family dinner' includes Alma? Is she a part of our family now?"

"Only if you want," Aunt Ruth responded. "But she's not a bad person and she seems to make Fred happy. I'm glad she's coming."

"I suppose it's good. It takes a lot to make him happy. Are my anti-war sentiments going to be part of the conversation?"

"I don't know. If your dad doesn't get on you, then I will. It is going to be dangerous out there. You can hold to your beliefs, but you need to sit this one out."

"Thanks for the warning. Does Uncle George have any inside information?"

"I'll ask him. Stay out of trouble, and I'll see you at dinner."

My Aunt Ruth and Uncle George owned three restaurants on the South Side of Chicago. Aunt Ruth was my dad's sister, but she had always been much closer to my mother. When Lizzie died, it was my aunt who sat at her bedside and cared for her while my dad was at work. My sister and I were in high school at the time.

Uncle George grew up in Chicago, where his family was active in politics. He had connections not given most people, which provided him with "other opportunities." He ran a bookie operation in the back room of his restaurant that police and politicians happily ignored. They were some of his best clients. George was also a Democratic Precinct Head in Mayor Daley's political machine, which made him a good person to know if there was going to be trouble.

When I got off the phone with Aunt Ruth, I went back to working on my résumé and setting up interviews. If Chicago didn't work, I would be forced to move back to Milwaukee to live with my dad. I shuddered at the thought. The only way to avoid it and get out of this crazy cycle of anxiety would be to get a job before my money ran out.

As a child I was afraid of my father, his anger being unpredictable and often unwarranted. My mother protected my sister and me from his rage, but there were times when an internal biological button was pushed, and all we could do was get out of the way. I remember an incident when I was about ten years old of breaking a glass pane in our front door. I was in a hurry and pushed my lunch pail through the glass. It shattered all around me.

"Mom!" I yelled in a panic, tears beginning to stream out of my eyes.

"What happened?" she asked, running toward me.

"I was late for the bus and broke the door. Dad is going to kill me. I didn't mean it. He's going to be so mad."

"Just get going. You're going to miss the bus."

All day I had knots in my stomach. I didn't eat any of my lunch, didn't listen to anything my teachers said, and withdrew from the games my friends were playing. I was so afraid of going home and facing my father.

Getting off the bus after school and running up the sidewalk, relief flooded over me when I saw there was no broken glass on the front stoop. The hole created by my lunch pail was gone and new glass replaced it.

"Mom!" I yelled. "What happened to the broken glass?"

"It was nothing," she said nonchalantly.

"Did you fix it?"

"It was easy. Now go get your homework done before supper."

My father never knew about my misdeed. My stomach

relaxed, and I stuffed myself at dinner, having avoided food all day. I was safe.

I was in high school when my mother passed, and I lost my protector. I was afraid I would not survive living with my father, but those fears were never realized, even though we still had a contentious relationship. I was unable to give him the father-daughter relationship he wanted, but I was mourning, too, and could not bridge the gap between my childhood fears and adult acceptance. It was a difficult time for our family and a constant struggle.

Now, getting ready for dinner at the Roadside Grill, I dressed in my most outrageous hippie style. I didn't want to blend in with the conservative Alma and my father, so I went full-on flower child. I braided my long blonde hair, leaving messy tendrils to frame my face. Bell-bottom pants topped with a peasant blouse and a fringed vest added to the look. A Pocahontas headband around my forehead and a hemp bag over my shoulder provided the perfect accessories to make a statement.

As I was getting ready, Sarah came into my room. "You really need to listen to the news," she said, turning on our old portable black-and-white TV.

"What's happening?" I asked.

"Tom Hayden was arrested in Lincoln Park for obstructing police, resisting arrest, and disorderly conduct. Everybody is marching to the Police station to protest his arrest. We need to join them now."

"I can't. I'm meeting my aunt and my dad for dinner."

"What time will it be over? You need to show up and support the cause."

"I'll get out as soon as I can, but it won't be until later. Where should we meet?"

"How about Grant Park at the statue of Major Jonathan Logan at nine o'clock."

The Roadhouse Grill was buzzing as I walked in and looked for my aunt. The barroom was crowded with people making toasts and pontificating about the merits of each candidate. Delegates wearing straw hats and covered with political buttons occupied every space and whether you supported Humphrey or McCarthy, you couldn't avoid the energy and enthusiasm of the crowd. They were boisterous, high energy, and ready for a fight on the political floor. I took a seat near the bar and felt the hum of the crowd crescendo like the incoming tide. The bar was designed for laughing, drinking games, boasting, and swearing, but tonight the talk was all politics. I was out of place with the anti-establishment vibe I was throwing off, but knowing I did not fit in with this group made me more determined to stay the course.

"Kim." My aunt motioned to me from across the room. "Over here."

I left the bar and walked into the restaurant to see my dad already sitting at a table with Alma. They both looked like typical Midwesterners, with their conservative clothes and haircuts, while I looked like I had just arrived from Haight Ashbury. Trying to mask his displeasure in front of Alma, my father narrowed his eyes and glared at me. "Nice clothes," he said. This was vintage Dad, not saying much but getting his point across.

"Hi, Dad," I said, ignoring his attitude and determined to get through this dinner. "How was the ride from Milwaukee?"

"Fine," he answered. "Alma and I left a little early to avoid traffic. We knew the city would be crowded with convention traffic."

"Fred," my aunt Ruth interrupted to keep the conversation on an even keel. "George wanted to join us tonight, but something came up and he is in the back room taking care of business."

"We'll miss him," said my dad as he looked around the restaurant trying to see into the back room. "I know Alma wanted to meet him and find out what exactly he does back there."

Everyone smiled because we all knew what George did in the back room. It wasn't a big secret that behind the scenes, Uncle George ran a bookie operation betting on the ponies. His wife, my aunt Ruth, was one of his biggest customers.

"I like your headband," Alma said, smiling at me with warmth and friendliness. She looked at my dad and I sensed genuine affection as I saw her squeeze his hand.

"Thank you, Alma." I answered with a sweet, smiling face matching the warmth of Alma. I was on best behavior and tried to further the conversation by saying, "I'm glad you could make the trip down here, especially with all of the commotion over the convention."

"I've been looking forward to this dinner to give us a chance to get caught up on what you're doing. How is your job search?"

I knew Alma was making attempts at friendliness, but the small talk was getting to me. I started talking louder and faster. "It's fine but I want to see what the democrats are going to do about this convention."

"Can we have a pleasant dinner and forget about politics for a night?" my aunt, the moderator, interrupted.

"Sounds good to me," I agreed, happy to end the conversation.

I knew Alma was a good person who made my dad happy, but there was something inside of me I could not get past. I liked her, but I resented her relationship with my dad, probably out of loyalty to my mother. I forced myself to be friendly toward her, but I knew I was acting badly. My parents never had a perfect marriage, maybe not even a good one, but when my mother got sick, my dad changed, and I saw how much he loved her. I once told him it was too bad she had to get sick to be noticed, and he recoiled from the impact of that statement. He neither defended himself nor mentioned the incident again. I suffered a guilty conscience for a long time, but I'm past that now.

The food at the Roadside Grill was delicious, and we spent an hour eating and talking about my job search and living in Chicago. We even lightly touched on the topic of presidential candidates. If a bystander watched the four of us, they'd see a typical family gathering, happily engaged in conversation and enjoying the evening out. They would not see a brother and sister who didn't get along, a widower with a new girlfriend, and a resentful daughter who was headstrong and rebellious.

Then the real purpose of the dinner started. "You aren't going to be in any of those protest marches, are you?" my dad asked, taking a final sip of his wine.

Grabbing my glass, I sipped my wine slowly, letting the liquid float over the surface of my mouth, sending tingling sensations to my head. The aroma relaxed me and gave me time to form a response. "Dad, you know I believe the war is wrong, and something has to be done to stop it."

"Those hippies are a bunch of anarchists and dropouts." My father became agitated, sucking in his breath and biting his lower lip. I'd seen this behavior too many times. "They should be arrested, and they probably will be before this is over. Let them sit in jail for a while and see how they feel about defaming their country. I don't want you to be a part of it."

I felt a tightening in my chest because I knew these demonstrations really mattered, but there was no way around his anger. I should not have fueled the fire, but I could not help it. "Dad," I said. "They call themselves Yuppies, and they're fighting for a cause I also believe in. If they get arrested, it's because the police and Mayor Daley don't grant them their civil liberties."

"That's bullshit." His voice rose above the hum of the other diners. "They're breaking the law, and you better not go near those demonstrations."

"You can't tell me what to do and I resent you even trying. You do not have authority over me."

"Okay," Aunt Ruth interjected while Alma sat passively staring at her glass of wine. "Fred, Kim is old enough to make her own decisions, but you are right in telling her not to go. George tells me Mayor Daley has orders to stop the demonstrators at all costs. Let's be done with this talk and have some dessert."

"I'm not done with it." I stare at my father, fists clenched, and my anger an acid burning in my stomach. I rejected the olive branch Aunt Ruth threw out and gritted my teeth to remain civil.

"I'm leaving now," I announced. "Thanks for dinner," I said to Ruth. To Alma, I said, "Aren't you glad you came?" Then I shot a glare at my father and left.

Once on the street, my rage bled through me, searching for a target for release. I went into a store to buy cigarettes and yelled at the clerk because she was not moving fast enough. Crossing the street, I gave oncoming cars the peace sign and made them stop to allow me to cross. And seeing a police officer talking to a motorist, I yelled, "Leave him alone!" There was no stopping this volcano from spewing its hot lava.

I was early for my rendezvous with Sarah, so I slowed my pace and tried to get control over my anger. I saw throngs of demonstrators already in Grant Park across from the Conrad Hilton Hotel, Humphrey's campaign center. This was the epicenter, the heart of the protest. More people were arriving from the north, their voices booming over loudspeakers. Hundreds of police in riot gear surrounded the area.

The crowd gathered momentum as more people joined the already growing volume of protesters. I crossed the street to add my support and was soon absorbed by the moving force, just one of a thousand bodies shouting, "Peace Now!" We were like a shoal of fish: one mass, one behavior, one mind, no free will. I fell in as a part of it.

The mass started to circle the monument of Civil War Major General Jonathan Logan. My commitment to the cause overrode my fear as I continued to feed off the energy of others. As the crowd circled, I felt a rush of emotion along with a confidence that I was participating in something with real meaning.

I looked to the statue and saw Sarah standing on one of the corners.

"Sarah!" I shouted above the noise of the crowd. "Over here!"

After I pushed my way through the crowd, we managed to connect. "We are making ourselves heard. The war needs to be stopped," I said, making my commitment clear.

Sarah was exuberant. "I told you this will be pivotal in the anti-war movement."

"What happened at the police station with Tom Hayden?"

"I don't know," said Sarah. "It was peaceful because I think they let him go. They know better than to incite this crowd with an unlawful arrest. It would be suicide."

"The dinner with my dad was like a suicide of my mind. He wanted to deaden my brain from free expression. I got out of there as quickly as I could."

"You need to be here to support this movement. This is your place." Sarah looked around. "I'm going to try to get closer to the statue to get a better view."

She took off, leaving me to follow her into the circling mob. On my right, I could see demonstrators climbing the statue of Major Logan and draping his horse with Viet Cong flags. They shouted obscenities at the police as the circle widened and the pace increased.

"Sarah, where are you?" I spoke.

Somehow, we got separated, and I was on my own in the middle of the mindless crowd. Someone passed by me, handing me a red banner, and telling me to move toward the statue. Waving the red banner, I shouted, "Ho, Ho, Ho Chi Minh!" My mind could only focus on the injustice and senselessness of the war. I marched and shouted.

That's when turmoil broke out. I was near the statue when the police rushed in, attempting to remove the protesters. A police officer pushed me aside and I fell into another demon-strator, both of us hitting the ground with force. I looked up and saw the statue covered with protesters, who were now kicking the police trying to hold their ground.

The police, better equipped, were able to dislodge the kids, except for one lone protester at the top of the statue. He raised his hands in a V and shouted, "Peace! Peace!" When the police reached him, he struggled, kicking, and trying to break free.

The police forcibly removed him by tugging and twisting his arms and, I'm sure, causing broken bones. I could hear him cry out in pain.

I remained on the ground and shouted into the crowd, "Leave him alone! He has a right to be there!"

A police officer near me glared and said, "He does not have that right. He's on public property."

"They still don't have to hurt him," I retorted.

"Think before you start yelling," he said, matching my anger with his own. "He caused this action by climbing up the statue. He gets what he deserves."

The injured boy was taken away, hopefully to a hospital. As shadows dissolved into nighttime, the crowd started to move away from the statue toward the Hilton Hotel. I fell into step with the advancing mob until I saw police with riot shields and full-face visors form a skirmish line to keep advancing protestors from crossing Michigan Avenue. They launched canisters of tear gas into the crowd, and the protestors retaliated by picking up bricks and empty cans to hurl back at them. This was not a fair fight, no honor, no code. Police advanced with Billy clubs in hand and brutality ensued. All this happened while cameras and videos recorded the incident.

Sarah was nowhere in sight and fear replaced my earlier convictions. I backed out of the crowd, looked one more time for Sarah, and left the scene.

The streets were void of traffic and eerily quiet except for the distant sound of sirens. The black air was thick and humid, its moisture mixed with my sweat to make my clothes cling. A gentle breeze did nothing to ease the stifling smell of anxiety. I felt like I was in a semi-trance as I walked to my apartment, only hearing the scuffing noise of my feet on the pavement.

Once home, I collapsed on the couch, my body still shaking from the events in the park. Sarah was not home and worrying about her added to my misery. I fell asleep watching the newscast, and sometime after midnight, Sarah came home, blood dripping down the side of her face. I took one look at her and saw my fears reflected in her face.

"Are you okay?" I stammered. I tried to hug her, but the vacant look she gave me was a warning not to advance. I saw red bruises forming on her arm as I ripped off her T-shirt. She would have large purple welts within the next few days.

"They're pigs out there who don't care about human rights and get pleasure out of the pain they inflict." Sarah spoke with passion and fervor.

"What happened?" I asked.

"I was trying to get away from the tear gas and one of the policemen grabbed and hit me. He raged and didn't care that he was hurting me. I swear I saw pleasure in his face."

"That can't be true," I said.

"Oh, believe it. You weren't there."

I took a deep breath to control my trembling voice. "Let me help you wash up and see if we need to do something about the cut above your eye. You know those things bleed like crazy, even if it's only a little scratch."

I walked Sarah into the bathroom and cleaned her wound. As I suspected, the cut was not deep and only needed a butterfly Band-Aid. I eased her into bed while she continued to rant on and on about unfairness and inhumane treatment, but once in bed, all her energy and bitterness evaporated, and she fell asleep.

The following day, my aunt called to check on me.

"Did my dad get home okay?" I asked after our initial greeting.

"You mean after your abrupt exit? Did you have to do that?" She sounded perturbed.

"Aunt Ruth, you know I can't deal with him telling me what I should and should not do. He thinks he still has authority over me, and he does not."

"Calm down, Kim," she said. "I understand your dad can be a little prickly, but he is doing it because he worries about you. He has issues of his own and doesn't want to add to them worrying about you. I have issues with Fred too, but I try to work around them!"

"I know," I responded. "Well, don't worry about me, because I'm staying home tonight. I need to set up some job interviews or my money will run out. At least I have your generous graduation gift to support me for a while!"

"Thanks, Kim. Glad I could help out," my aunt said. "Good luck."

———

The third night of the convention determined the Democratic candidate for President. More violence would probably follow more protests. I shuddered as I remembered the scene at Major Logan's statue, but I also felt the ever-present pull of my convictions. Sarah, recovering from her injury, was planning to go to Grant Park where thousands of people were assembling to await the results of the balloting. McCarthy was considered the anti-war candidate, and a victory for him symbolized a victory for the protests.

By four o'clock, Sarah was home, changing her clothes, and heading out to the demonstration.

"Why don't you come with me?" she said.

"I can't," I explained, using the same excuse I'd used the night before. "I need to do more work to prepare for my interviews."

"Screw them," Sarah retorted. "If this world falls apart, there will be no interviews or future for anyone."

"I promised my aunt I wouldn't get involved."

"You're running out of excuses. That last one is lame," Sarah said convincingly. "Besides, the demonstration tonight is permitted by Mayor Daley, so there shouldn't be as much trouble."

"How do you know that? I think as long as the war goes on, there will always be trouble."

"True," Sarah said with a sigh. "But tonight will be better. The police have gotten so much flack about their brutality, they will tone it down for tonight. The beatings have been broadcast on the screens in the convention hall, so everybody knows about their viciousness. The public is on our side."

"Okay, I'm with you, but only as an observer."

"That's great," Sarah said, sounding pleased with herself. "I'm meeting friends at the northwest corner of the grandstand in Grant Park. You can come along. It'll be safe."

I changed clothes into my worn-out blue jeans that felt like rebellion. To get an extra measure of security, I put my lucky gold coin in my back pocket to keep me safe. The coin was given to me by my mother before she passed, and she told me it always brought her safely home.

We got to the bandstand early and waited for Sarah's friends. The crowd was talking about the convention voting down the peace resolution, and how our government was failing us. The noise level began to rise, and the surrounding sounds became charged with a negative intensity. The rage of the protesters bled into me, and I cursed myself for letting Sarah talk me into this. I was afraid of police brutality, but also afraid of the actions of the mob. This was not good.

"Hell no, we won't go!" someone shouted from a huge megaphone. The chant engulfed everyone with its rhythmic vibration.

"Hell no, we won't go!"

"Hell no, we won't go!"

I climbed up the corner of the bandstand to find a safe place. The raised view allowed me to see the incredible number of people becoming incited by the chant. They seemed oblivious to the dangers closing in on them.

A boy wearing an army helmet climbed up a flagpole and reached for the halyard so he could lower the flag. The crowd near him began shouting, "Tear down the flag!"

Protestors around me became volatile, threatening, and I jumped off the bandstand to get out of their way. As I wound my way through the crowd, I passed close to the flagpole and saw one white-shirted police officer and two blue-shirted policemen at the base, waiting for the boy to climb down. I looked up and saw the youth, so passionate in his motives, exercising his right to do what he knew was morally the right thing. As he climbed down, he was immediately arrested, which set off a new round of shouting.

"Pigs! Pigs!"

Objects from the ground—rocks, cans, bottles—everything was thrown at the retreating police. Another youth ran to the flagpole with a red cloth, maybe long underwear, and climbed the pole to attach the symbol of the Viet Cong flag at half-mast.

All I wanted was to get away from the frenzied crowd. I had my beliefs, like the other demonstrators, but mob behavior was preventing reasonable action. Out of the corner of my eye,

I saw a row of police in riot gear advance toward the flagpole, clubbing and beating anyone in their way. I was looking for a way out when I saw Sarah.

"Over here!" I yelled. "Sarah, watch out!" I shouted a warning, but it was too late. A police officer came from behind and struck her arm, causing her to fall to the ground. She put her arms over her head for protection but to no avail. He hit her again and again.

I was horrified and had to get her out of there before she was seriously beaten or arrested. She probably needed medical attention. Running toward her, I headed right into the middle of the action, focused only on getting both of us out of this mess and home to safety. Pushing my way forward, I could not see what was behind me, and a police officer closed in and roughly seized my arm and struck me in the back.

"No!" I shouted. "I'm not a part of this! I only want to get my friend home."

"You should have thought about that before you started shouting and throwing things."

"I didn't throw anything!"

I started crying hysterically. I turned around to plead with the officer, but as I turned, he got hit in the leg with a brick and screamed in pain.

"Get out of here!" someone yelled at me from out of no-where. I was so dazed; I didn't heed the warning and couldn't move.

I felt something clutch my ankle and hold it in place. It was the injured policeman, still lying on the ground but preventing my escape. He pushed me down as his rage exploded. I fell face-first to the ground. When I opened my eyes, all I could see were glossy strands of green trampled into the dark molasses earth. I buried my head in my arms and began to sob.

The police officer regained his stability and grabbed me by my back pocket. Twisting away from him, I heard my pocket rip and worried about my coin. Rolling over, I caught a glimpse of his face under his riot helmet and saw bruises on his cheek and cold, narrow eyes. He looked at me as if I was some approaching enemy, ready to harm anything in the way.

Grabbing my already-sore arm without any concern for my well-being, the officer pulled me up and forced my hands behind my back. After he snapped on a pair of handcuffs, he pushed me forward through the jeering crowd, and all I heard were taunts and mocking insults thrown at him. "Wait!" I shouted above the roar of the crowds. "My coin! I lost my coin when you tore my pocket. I need to find it."

"No way," he said, giving me another push. I stumbled and fell again. "Get up and get going," he commanded.

"No!" I yelled, surprised at the vehemence in my voice. "That coin is a memento given to me by my dying mother. Don't you have any compassion? Or do you even *have* a mother? Do you have a heart, or any kind of humanity? It's the only thing I have left from her."

I became hysterical, ranting on and on but refusing to move. My voice was raspy, and my thoughts fragmented, but I kept a constant stream of gibberish going until I noticed the officer's mean eyes soften, and his anger dissipate.

"Okay," he said.

He pushed me, a little more gently, back to the spot where I initially fell, and before long, I saw the shiny spot of gold tucked under the blades of grass. No one else had seen it, and when I asked the police officer to please pick it up, he obliged.

"But you're still going to jail," he said, only slightly softer.

At one point, I looked behind to find Sarah, but she was nowhere in sight. The police had surrounded the flagpole to clear the crowd and most of the protesters moved on. I struggled a little, mostly a knee-jerk reaction, but my arresting officer felt my muscles twitch and tightened his grip.

"I did you a favor, now you cooperate," he said. Resigned to the fact that I was going to jail, I cooperated.

An armored patrol wagon nearby was stationed to take demonstrators to jail. I was told to get in, sit down, and wait. Two men were already sitting in the back, and I took a seat on an uncomfortable metal bench as far away from them as possible. One of the men had a gash on his head, and the other appeared drugged into a stupor. I did not talk to either of them. Finally, when the van was nearly filled, the police added two more female protesters and locked the door. "We were just standing there," one of the women said. "We did nothing,"

Battered hippies, stoned protesters, and misfits like me waited for the van to leave. The women, who were now laying on the floor, rambled on. "Two policemen came right up behind us, slammed us to the ground, and put handcuffs on our wrists. The cuffs were tight and cut off my circulation. My wrists were swollen and bruised. "This isn't fair."

"Join the crowd," yelled someone from the back.

"Your story sounds like mine," I said, looking at the girls. Blood was dripping from their noses and scratches covered their arms and legs. One had a large bruise forming on her forehead. Neither looked as if they had a bath or clean clothes in several days. They were completely stoned and did not look like innocent bystanders.

"Do you know what happens next?" I asked.

"I've been through this before," replied the first girl, who was at least somewhat coherent. "Those pigs will just hold us for a little while to scare us. Nothing will happen because we did nothing wrong."

"Peace to you," said someone from the back, holding his arms up in a victory salute.

The van finally took off and sped down Michigan Avenue, making several sharp turns along the way. None of us had seat belts, and our hands were cuffed behind our backs, so we couldn't brace ourselves around the turns. I fell to the floor at one point, sustaining more bruises and adding insult to an already humiliating experience.

We arrived at the District One headquarters and waited in line for the police to complete their paperwork and process us: names, addresses, and birthdays. A holding tank was the next stop, and it was filled with other protesters. There were no windows, no creature comforts, and not even a clock to know how long we had been there. It was noisy and smelly, and someone was banging on the wall non-stop insisting his constitutional rights had been violated. Everyone in the cell was young, ragged, bruised, and insolent, talking about getting out so they could fight "the pigs." I just wanted to get out and go home.

For the next seven hours, I was not read my rights, not allowed to make a phone call, and not told what I was charged with. Eventually, stale cheese sandwiches were passed around to anyone who wanted them, but I couldn't eat.

"You should eat that," one of the other detainees said.

"I can't," I said. "I think I'll throw up."

"Well, you shouldn't be in here long," she said with optimism.

"Do you know what's going to happen?" I asked her.

"You'll either be fined with a violation or released. They can't put all of us in jail. After all, this is Cook County. They don't have room."

More arrests followed, and each new person entering the

holding tank told stories of police violence and tear gas on Michigan Avenue.

"I thought we had freedom of speech in this country," a new detainee shouted after being pushed into the holding tank. He clutched a badly bruised arm and shouted, "Where are my civil liberties?"

"Gone when you break the law," the police officer said as he slammed the door shut, locking everyone inside.

"What's the latest out there?" I asked after the police officer left.

"Everything is out of control. All along Michigan Avenue there are beatings, and innocent people being arrested and carted off by an out-of-control police force."

He sat on the floor next to the girl who was mumbling something incoherent about war. He looked at her in disgust and continued, "The pigs are using tear gas, and a lot of people are sick and coughing." He looked at me and said, "You look okay. Why are you in here?"

"I got mixed up in the mess. I was in the wrong place at the wrong time," I told him.

"That's what they all say." The girl on the floor perked up. "I want to get out of here."

"You will eventually," I told her, even though she probably should stay the night, just to keep her safe.

The detainees continued to commiserate. "Did you expect this kind of violence?" I asked the guy sitting on the floor.

"The pigs forced us. They're the violent ones. We have freedom of speech on our side."

"I thought tonight was permitted," said the boy with the bruised arm standing across from me. "My arm is paying the price for protecting my rights."

"It's all their fault," someone else from the corner chimed in. "This violence is on them, not us."

"Our rights were violated," said the boy, clutching his injured arm.

I sat silently in a corner of the cell, afraid to say anything to this angry group. The girl on the floor raised her head one more time and said, "I want to get out of here. Can you get me out of here?" She looked around the room and when no one responded, she laid her head on her arm and passed out.

At four a.m., I was allowed to make a phone call. Escorted past the station's control room, I saw anxious parents, distraught friends, and ragged protestors, all waiting in long lines. At every desk, police busied themselves with documenting personal information, filling out forms and trying to answer people's questions. Frustration was high, and I saw one person lose their cool and was removed to someplace else. I don't know where.

I got to the phone banks but had to wait for a half hour before one became available. I dialed with shaking fingers.

"Aunt Ruth, it's Kim."

There was silence on the other end of the phone line until I heard Aunt Ruth utter, "What, Kim? Do you know what time it is?"

"Yes, I do," I responded. "Aunt Ruth, I'm in jail and I need help."

"Kim, I warned you." Another pause. "Are you okay?"

"I'm a little bruised, but I'm mostly just tired. I've been held at the police station for more than seven hours."

"What did you do?" my aunt asked.

"I'll explain everything later. Can you get me out of here?"

"Have you been charged with anything?"

"Not yet. That's why I want to get out."

"I'll be there as soon as I can," said Aunt Ruth, hanging up.

Waiting for my aunt, I studied the commotion around me. It was controlled chaos with pockets of shouting, some yelling anti-war slogans, and others pleading for clemency. I sat next to an office with the name Chief Max Doherty stenciled on the window. I watched detainees and families go in and out of the door, some leaving relieved, and others ushered back to their cells, nobody was happy.

Finally, it was my turn to enter the chief's office. He was sitting at his desk, poring over some reports, looking frustrated and tired. I guessed he was around fifty; he looked weathered from years in the field and an aura of gloom surrounded him. Family pictures lined the shelf behind him. I hoped I was looking into the face of a father who could understand pain and children and maybe give me a break.

"What do you want?" he growled at me, sounding as if his voice was made of leather.

"Hi, my name is Kim Weber, and I was improperly arrested last night. I was not involved in any violence."

"But you were there, and this paper in front of me says you resisted arrest and hit an officer."

"That is only partially true," I responded. "I actually lost a special coin when a police officer pushed me down, and I needed to get it back."

There was a knock on the door and my aunt entered the office.

"Well, well, Ruth," said a now-delighted Max.

Aunt Ruth walked over to Max, gave him a hug, and looked at me with a questioning glance.

"Do you two know each other?" I asked.

Ruth nodded. "We haven't seen you at the restaurant in a few weeks," she said to Max. "I hope all of this trouble isn't keeping you away from us."

"No, it never will. Just slows down my extracurricular activities!" After more small talk, Max said "So, what can I do for you, Ruth?"

"Kim is my niece, and she got herself arrested at one of the demonstrations. I thought you might help her out."

"Isn't it funny? I was just looking at her paperwork and thinking how a nice girl like her got tangled up in this mess." Max shot me a warning grin to keep my mouth shut.

"She's a great kid that only recently moved to Chicago to find a job. She got caught up in the moment." My aunt returned the knowing smile back to Max.

"I'll see what I can do. Anything for you, Ruth."

Aunt Ruth and I left the office, filled out release forms, and exited the police station. Once outside I cried, only stopping to catch another breath so I could continue crying with more vehemence. When my racking sobs finally ended and my tension dissipated, I turned to my aunt and squeezed her so tight she could barely breathe.

"I'm sorry," I blubbered. "I'm usually good in a crisis, but after it's resolved, I go to pieces. How can I ever thank you for getting me out of there?"

"I'm happy to help and glad it was Max who was in control. He has a penchant for the ponies, so George knows him well and I've talked to him a few times at the restaurant."

I could feel a shift in the tone of my aunt's voice, her stress ebbing as we walked away from the police station. She did not reprehend me for my foolishness but talked of understanding and coping. She wrapped her arm around my shoulder and pulled me close. Moments like this reminded me of my mother, my protector, who always saw the best side of me, even when I screwed up.

I wanted to explain, "I was so angry with the policeman who arrested me. I was trying to find my friend and he grabbed me and ripped my back pocket. My coin fell out of my pocket."

"I know the coin you are referring to."

"I thought it was lost but he let me go back to find it."

"Not all police officers are bad."

"My mother gave me that coin as a legacy of our family through good and bad times. It wasn't always lucky, but it was always something cherished. I can't lose another part of her."

My aunt's face shimmered in the glow of the early morning light. She was crying.

ROUND FIVE

KIM

APRIL 19, 2009

My head has been spinning with reflections on my turbulent youth. All that chaos around me, and as much frustration as my family had brought me, the one totem I feared losing was the family coin. Losing was never my game. No wonder I keep hoping to find clues about myself in my family's past.

Round 5 is complete and no new disaster has surfaced. I have more energy, so Mark and I take walks on the groomed hiking trails near our house. They provide exercise without exhausting my energy.

We live in the Kettle Moraine area of Wisconsin, named for the kettles and moraines left by glaciers two and a half million years ago. We often hike along its many trails and the path we follow today is woven between ancient tree roots and new wood chips. It is hilly, but not so taxing that I become out of breath when climbing the slopes. Birds sing and light filters through a canopy of leaves, creating a kaleidoscope of designs and sounds that sing to my soul. Along the path are fallen acorn shells, their skin crumbled and decorated with lichen. The scent of pine fills the air and is fresh and cleansing. I breathe it into my lungs.

Mark and I pause and listen to the gusty wind blowing through the fluttering leaves above. I look up into the canopy and become hypnotized by the leaves, which now appear thick and dense, like hundreds of eyes watching me. They form a cage around me. I feel entwined. It makes me uneasy, and I shudder.

"What's the matter?" asks Mark. "I thought you were enjoying this walk."

"I am," I say. "It's just suddenly, I feel trapped in the woods. It's beautiful but I want to get out."

"Let's turn around and head back to the car. It's about a fifteen-minute walk."

As we retrace our steps, I say, "I want to talk about what happens if I don't make it through this illness."

Mark slows his pace and looks uncomfortable, his normal upright posture shrinking as he slumps forward. "We don't need to talk about this now," he says without looking at me.

"Yes, we do. The family needs a way to say goodbye and move on after I pass. You will need to do the same."

"You're doing so well with your treatment. We can talk about this later."

"You're wrong." I'm impatient and no longer have the time for meaningless conversations. I steel myself against his denial and force the conversation again. Gritting my teeth, I say, "The best time to talk about death is when it's not imminent. I want the family to know what possibilities exist. I don't want them to experience guilt the way I did when my mother died."

Mark, still not hearing the pain in my voice, says, "Nobody will feel guilty. You have made a lot of good things happen."

"Maybe." I control my breath, trying to loosen my body movements, but my hands remain clenched. "I am not afraid of dying. I don't need to mend any bridges. I just want to be prepared."

Ignoring my comment, Mark continues, "Everyone will miss you terribly, and there will be a gap in all of our lives." His voice is trembling as he glances at my white-knuckled hands. "Let's deal with this later, after we know the results of the treatment."

My suppressed anger rises to the surface. "We already know the result of the treatment. The result is uncertainty."

"I mean, we need to know if you are in remission."

"Remission isn't important now." Mark is not understanding the point. "I want the family to know I am happy and not remorseful about my end. I want to be able to talk about death while I still have my faculties and can speak rationally. I told you how guilty I felt after my mother died. I don't want that for you or anyone else."

"You can't control how others feel. You can't take away our grief by saying everything is okay because it's not."

"All I'm saying is that you will need closure after I'm gone. I didn't have it with my mother, and it took soul-searching before I got to a point of acceptance. I don't think I'll ever have closure with Billy, and I don't want that for the family."

"Billy's death took a lot out of both of us," Mark says as he looks away in sadness, focusing on some obscure plant that has nothing to do with anything.

"You never talk about Billy," I say, stopping our walk and forcing eye contact. Mark's face is the blank canvas of denial. That canvas holds all the colors and textures of a work of art, but nothing is visible. I know there is a lot hidden inside.

I shake my head, hoping to clear my thoughts and make one more attempt at getting through to Mark. "I know Billy's loss devastated you and sent me into an unimaginable depression. I feel cancer is my last chapter."

"Kim, I don't want to hear about this anymore. Last time you let it slip that you were losing your will to live, but I can't accept that. I can't let you give up." Mark picks up his pace, each footfall chaotically spaced from the last as if in confusion. He adds, "I cannot let you think this way."

"Mark, can you please slow down so we can talk?"

When he turns around to allow me to catch up, I see tears in his eyes, unnoticed, but visible to me.

"You are living in denial, both with Billy's death and my cancer," I state with finality. "We have to have this conversation. I'm not a religious person, so I don't know if I will go to heaven or hell, be reincarnated as some animal, or become a ghost. I want to make my passing easy on you and the rest of the family."

"There will be nothing easy about your passing. You are a force, the glue holding everyone together, and everyone will mourn no matter what you say about living a good life."

This comment takes me aback. Did I have happiness, joy, and a sense of purpose? Did I have a good life? I was so brave when I was a teenager. I really stood my ground. It's all I've ever done since. My mind goes back in time but always stops with Billy. What glue should I have used to hold him to me? What force should I have drawn upon to prevent his death? Did Billy have a good life? I'm not sure.

"Final chapters are always sad," I say, trying to put my thoughts of Billy out of my mind.

"Don't think about that now," Mark says.

"I want to be cremated in a simple ceremony, family only. If you want, you can have a celebration of life later."

Mark nods, unable to respond.

"I want my ashes spread in three places," I say. "Some in the lake, where we spent so many happy years; some on my parents' gravesite; and some planting a Japanese maple in a location of your choice, protected from the winter wind. I think the family will be happy with that. I know I will."

"I can do all of that," Mark says as he wraps his arm around me in tenderness. A slight wind picks up and the trees flutter, releasing the cage around me. "Do you still want to get out of these woods?"

I release myself from Mark's embrace, not in anger, but with the intent of creating a space between us that can be filled with understanding. "I want to go home. I want to be prepared. I want dignity. I want you to hold me and remember me as your loving wife. I need to live on in the hearts of my family."

"There is no question your spirit will live for generations. Look at your ancestors and what you learned from their struggles. They were strong and so are you. Your descendants will know you and the world you created for them."

"Thank you for this."

Mark and I walk in silence for a while until we decide to take a shortcut back to our car. The path narrows and becomes rocky. Since my strength and balance are still weak, I have difficulty with the rougher terrain and I stumble, falling to my knees. Mark runs up to me in a panic, asking if I'm hurt, but I turn to him and laugh.

"Nothing like a fall to break the tension. I'm such a klutz," I say, trying to recover some dignity. "My head is so full of serious thoughts. I didn't take time to look at what's in front of me. I need to ease up and laugh more."

"I'm not laughing until I'm sure you are not hurt."

"You can laugh, I'm okay. Probably just a skinned knee. You know the story of the skinned knee. It's a metaphor for learning your lesson."

Mark finally laughs.

THERAPY

KIM
SEPTEMBER 2001

D riving to work along the beautiful Lake Michigan shoreline has a way of freeing my mind from tension. Today, the lake is helping me prepare for my day by giving me rainbow rays of morning light that dance across the water. It relaxes my mind and body and makes me a more effective therapist. I am seeing a difficult patient and I need to be at the top of my game.

Traffic is light, so my mind wanders to last night's dinner when Mark and I talked about our winter vacation.

"Where do you want to go this year to escape the cold weather?" I asked him.

"Should we try a new continent?" he answered.

"That gives us several choices. We've already been to Europe and Asia."

"You can choose," Mark said. "Anything except Antarctica!"

"Are you telling me you don't want to brave any cold weather, even if you get to see penguins?"

Mark's scowling eyes tease me with disagreement.

Having been together for many years, Mark and I understand the ins and outs of each other's personalities. We started our marriage the right way, as friends before lovers, and in time, those feelings became so strong that each of us would sacrifice for the well-being of the other. Sex was the bonus.

I remember everything about the night we met. I was having a drink with one of my colleagues at a local bar, listening to the problem she was having in her marriage. Her husband was in sales for his father's company and was often gone in the evenings entertaining clients, or so he said. Somehow, her husband tracked her down at the bar that night and created an embarrassing scene, yelling accusations and pounding his fists until both stormed out, leaving me alone with my face red as a beet. I didn't realize someone on the other side of the bar was watching the entire scene, and for some reason, decided I needed rescuing, or at least a friend. He introduced himself, we talked for hours, and that was the start of our romance.

Mark and I were compatible right from the beginning, even though we were different in many ways. I am tall and blonde; Mark is muscular with dark curly hair. He is a left-brained person, good with numbers and logic, whereas I am right-brained, good with emotions and feelings. In our marriage, he is the head and I am the heart, although those lines are easily breached.

When we met, I had recently moved to Milwaukee from Chicago. I needed a change of environment, not to mention wanting to return to the familiar places where I had grown up. Chicago had too many bad memories. First there was the 1968 riots, then I couldn't find a job, and finally I came to the disappointing realization that I needed an advanced degree to have the career I sought. Two more long years of schooling spent in the heart of the windy city, listening to constant horns blaring, sirens screeching, and living in tiny spaces. I was done with Chicago.

I think back now to the early years of our marriage, the years before our son was born. Ours was a union of peers, equal partners in a commitment to a future together. When I first became pregnant, we knew one of us had to put their career on hold, and I wanted to be that person. I wanted the luxury of time so I could focus on my baby, have him by my side, and sit under the sky in the warm grass and sing lullabies. I got all that while Billy was young, but once he reached school age, I grew restless and went back to my career.

———————

As I near my office the rainbow rays are still shimmering on Lake Michigan. My office, where I see private clients, is near downtown, but not in a conventional office building. I found my space in a hundred-year-old Victorian mansion converted into offices. The exterior construction is cream city brick, typical of that era, and details like towers, turrets, dormers, and a mix of ornate trim gives a gingerbread effect to the mansion. I love it. A huge Queen Anne wraparound porch invites people to sit and relax on the comfortable Adirondack chairs where they can watch bikers and joggers travel before them in the park across the street.

Walking up the curved sidewalk to the front door, I read the plaque on the outside brick: "Kim Weber, Psychologist." Inside, my office is bright and airy with views of Lake Michigan and a park. Since it's September, the grass is still green and the sky a deep blue, but some of the maple trees are starting to turn yellow. By October, they'll be bright crimson. Behind my building is a large, modern hospital overlooking the same scene. It is the juxtaposition of the two architectural styles that make this area unique, a place where old meets new.

Once inside my office, I review the case files for my first patient. Peter is a thirty-eight-year-old father of two who lost his wife more than a year ago in an automobile accident. He suffers from complicated grief, an adjustment disorder that interferes with his normal, everyday functioning.

Peter enters my office and sits across from me, his hands clenched so tight they pinch his skin. He is nervous and tense.

"Can I get you something to drink?" I ask.

"I'll take a glass of water. I don't want to eat."

I give Peter a glass of water. "I'm glad you could make it in today. Did you have trouble getting your kids ready for school this morning?"

"Yes," he says. "I dropped them off a few minutes ago. They should be glad they have a ride to school, but they're not. All they do is argue."

Peter's speech is rapid, and he is clasping and unclasping his hands in a rhythmic pattern. He hesitates a moment, as if unsure of himself, and says, "I want to talk about my wife, Jean, because I think she would be very unhappy with the events of last week."

"You mean the bombing of the World Trade Center?"

Peter nods.

"What makes you think Jean is upset?"

"She wants to be here to find a way to protect our boys."

"Aren't you protecting them?"

"Maybe, but I know she doesn't think I'm doing enough. She would insist we move out of the city to get away from danger. I need her help in making decisions about our kids."

"Peter, neither you nor your boys are in immediate danger. I would caution you not to make a drastic change in your life right now. How do you know Jean feels this way?"

"She tells me things. She's watching me to be sure I do the right thing."

Peter took a sip of water and tried to calm himself by looking outside. It was a cloudless, beautiful day, but that does not calm his anxiety. I have never seen him so nervous.

"Don't you have someone in your life you want to please?" Peter said with a penetrating stare and an accusatory tone in his voice. "Someone who is gone but still with you?"

"Peter, we have to focus on your situation. It's not unusual to want to talk to Jean, or ask her advice, but you have to make the decisions on your own."

"Don't you know that's what I'm trying to do?" Peter got up and walked to the window. His hands once again opened and closed rhythmically. "I know she died in a car accident, but her presence is inside of me. She talks to me in my head."

"It's been over a year since Jean passed. You will always love and remember her, but you must focus on how to go on with your life."

Peter returns to the chair and slumps into its comfort. He puts his hands in his pockets and examines a dust spot on the floor. After an uncomfortable moment, his eyes wander up to the ceiling and his feet rapidly tap the floor.

"You don't know what you're talking about." Peter's anger bursts forth. "I came here for help because I was depressed, but you are trying to convince me I'm crazy."

Peter gets up again and starts to move around the room like his insides are propelling him in all directions. His eyes are wild, and he moves to a chair in the opposite corner where he starts rocking, rocking, faster and faster. Suddenly, he is talking, words crowded together, and sentences fragmented, as if he is in a mental free-fall.

"Peter," I shout, but he doesn't hear me, or doesn't want to hear me. He continues rocking and babbling. I go over to him and put my hand on his back.

Looking up at me, he says, "You don't know anything."

"Peter," I respond, "come back and sit down."

He follows me back to my desk, sits, and stares out the window. "You don't know how it feels to lose someone who has been the center of your life. You can't tell me Jean isn't still with me. I need her. I don't need you and I don't need your psychobabble."

Giving Peter a moment, I try to continue. "I wanted you to understand that the pleasure you take in talking to Jean is only masking the pain you feel from her loss."

"I want to be angry," Peter is adamant. "I want to feel something other than helpless. When I go into the bathroom, her makeup and lotions are scattered on the vanity, but she is not there; in the kitchen, her vitamins rest on the windowsill, but she is not there; I can't go into her closet because I smell her presence, but she is not there; my boys want the same breakfast their mom made, but Jean is not there to prepare it. She envelops me with her presence, but she is not physically there. The only time I am happy is when we talk, and even though she is not there, I feel her inside me. I don't want you to take that away from me, and I resent you even trying."

"I am not trying to take her away," I respond with firmness, maintaining a steady gaze. "I'm trying to help you find a way to deal with her loss. Your boys need you."

"I don't want to move forward. I want Jean. You sit in your comfortable chair doling out advice, but you don't know what it's like to lose everything." Peter's voice is bitter, and he continues to fidget as tension returns to his face. His breathing becomes more rapid, shallower as the personal storm inside him threatens to erupt.

"I do know you're hurting, and I can offer ideas that may help. Right now, your anger is clouding your thinking. You need to relax."

Peter's glare softens but his face remains tense. He closes his eyes, slows his breathing, and takes a long, deep breath.

After a few moments of silence, Peter relaxes enough to avert another panic attack.

"Do you think you need the constant reminders of Jean in your house, such as her makeup or her pills? Do you think you could remove some of her personal items without letting go of her presence?"

"I tried once to throw away her makeup. I felt she didn't need it anyway, because she was already beautiful, but I never got around to doing it. I could try that."

"Good," I say. "That's a start."

Driving home that evening, I'm still troubled by Peter's outburst. A patient has never accused me of not knowing what I was doing. I must admit, he hit a nerve and I need to think about everything he said. I find Mark relaxing in our study.

"I know we have an unspoken rule," I say, interrupting his peaceful contemplation, "that we do not give professional advice to each other, but I'm really troubled by one of my patients. He suffers from complicated grief due to the death of his wife, and he accused me of not understanding because I have never gone through it."

Mark looks a little perplexed. "You don't need to lose a spouse or child to understand grief," he says. "I didn't know you when your mother was sick, but I understand being a caretaker of a dying parent causes grief."

"That's not the same as complicated grief. I got over it, he has not. He fantasizes that he is still talking to her."

"You mean he's psychotic?"

"I don't think so. It's just the pleasure-pain syndrome. The bombing of the World Trade Center heightened his anxiety and made his fantasy world more appealing."

"My fantasies are always more appealing." Mark tries to lighten the mood, but when he sees I'm still troubled, he continues. "When your mother died, you had healthy grief. You loved her but learned to deal with her loss. Your client needs to get to that point. Don't doubt yourself or your ability to help."

"You're probably right," I say, sounding less certain than I would like.

"On the brighter side," Mark says, changing the subject, "Billy called and he's coming home from school this weekend. A couple of his classes were cancelled, so he'll be here Wednesday. I have a dinner meeting that night, but you can go out with him and have a nice dinner together."

"That does brighten my day. I haven't talked to him since the day he called about 9/11. It will be good to catch up."

Billy has always been the focus of Mark's and my life. Physically, he is a miniature Mark—wild, curly black hair and hazel eyes that melt all the colors of autumn into a single hue. We protect him with our love, stand by him in times of danger, allow him to fly when he becomes a man. A spark was in his eyes from birth and whatever challenges he may face, we understand the boy inside, the one that is Billy. I love him totally.

"We're going to the Tasty Thrill for dinner," I say, greeting Billy as he walks through the door, duffel bag in hand. He has the hungry look of a college student who needs some good food.

"Is Dad coming too?"

"He has a meeting, but he'll join us later."

"Good," Billy says.

The Tasty Thrill is a burger joint that also has healthy fare on its menu. Neither of us like chain restaurants or bars, so this fits our needs with good food and quiet crowds. The atmosphere is bright, airy, and filled with the aroma of garlic and onions as well as Indian spices like turmeric, cumin, and ginger. We both love it, but as a sizzling plate of something spicy whiffs past me, my eyes begin to water.

"Mom," Billy says. "Are you allergic to something, or so happy to be with me that you're crying?"

"A little of each, I guess."

We each order a grilled seafood special and fall into easy conversation. Billy says school is going well and he's made a lot of new friends. The relaxed tone of his voice is soothing and sweeps away my worries. It is a joy to be with him. Then he brings up calculus.

"I'm having trouble in my calc class. I got a B minus on my first test."

"That's not bad. Don't worry about it."

"I know, but I need to keep my grades up so I can get into a graduate program. Dad was the first person to pass five actuarial exams before graduating and you're a psychologist. You guys set a tough precedent for me to live up to."

"Not really. Your dad has always been focused, but it took me a long time to get my act together. Don't even ask me about my hippie days."

As we talk, I watch Billy unconsciously drumming his fingers on the table. I see his nails chewed down to the cuticle and even though he looks relaxed, nervousness resides within him. I am his mother and I know him so well.

"I know all about your hippie days," Billy smiles at me with teasing charm.

"It takes a long time to achieve confidence," I reassure Billy, "even now I sometimes question my abilities. You can help me with a client I'm working with. I'll tell you about him without using his name."

I explain the confrontation with Peter. I told him it upset me because he questioned my ability to treat him.

Billy appears surprised when I confess my insecurities. "I see what you're talking about, but you've had grief in your life, especially as a teenager when your mom died. I wasn't there, but I don't think you created a fantasy like your patient. You didn't stop living because of that tragedy."

"No, I definitely did not stop living."

"Maybe you had the opposite reaction. Maybe your grief drove you into your rebellious lifestyle during the sixties. You were lost, but he is lost in a different way."

I think about this. I was a mess after my mother died, and maybe it was complicated grief or maybe it was ordinary teenage rebellion. I marvel at how intuitive Billy is.

"What sort of things bother you?" I ask Billy, expecting a generic response to a typical parent question.

Billy appears confused and focused on something behind my head. His lips become pursed but remain slightly open, allowing the air to flow in and out in waves. After a moment, he blinks and turns his focus to me.

"I sometimes have a voice in my head telling me to do things, not bad things, but just choices. An instant later, I blank out and when I can refocus, I have forgotten what I was supposed to do," Billy looks troubled and calls the waiter for another glass of water.

"What do you mean?" I ask. "You have the confidence to make decisions. I worry that sometimes you are too serious."

"That's how you see me, but I'm different on the inside. I'm scattered and have trouble keeping track of what I'm supposed to do. I forget a lot of stuff."

I'm perplexed by Billy's comment. There is a stirring in my head that tells me I'm missing something. I look at Billy and see a loving son, but my instincts are firing inside my head, telling me something is wrong.

"I've never known you to be forgetful. You are a rule-follower and make good decisions. Is this about the B minus on your calc test? That's not bad."

"It's not that, although next time I'm going to study my buns off. I worry about the way I constantly dwell on my problems. They're always on my mind and I can't get past it."

The food arrives. The sight and aroma of our dinner takes us away from our discussion and into the world of sensory delights. Problems dissolve like the hot butter on our rolls, and my salmon and Billy's fillet provide the comfort we need.

"Let's put aside our problems for now and talk about them later," I say as we dive into our dinner.

Arriving at my office early the next morning, I start to research complicated grief as well as the memory issue Billy talked about at dinner last night. My library fits the Victorian design of the building and has a wall of floor-to-ceiling shelves with room for hundreds of books. I fill less than half of the shelves with the old, musty textbooks of my college days. Most of my research comes from the countless journals and case studies I subscribe to which offer current information and diagnosis. I place a stack of newer journals on my desk and start reading.

Billy's comments last night took me by surprise, and we didn't talk about it later as I had promised. The articles I read in my journals said that temporary forgetfulness or even confusion are typical in teenagers if they are short-term and not affecting normal life. Since I never actually observed Billy having a problem, I dismiss it as a phase college kids go through. My concerns from last night are unfounded.

Turning to my treatment of Peter, I read the latest research on complicated grief. The more I read, the more disturbed I become; not because of Peter but because of a similar pattern I see in my life. Do I suffer from complicated grief about the death of my mother, even though it happened a long time ago? Did I ever get closure? This idea troubles me.

———————————

Over the next two months, Peter cancels several appointments and attempts to contact him result in unanswered emails and unresponsive voicemails. Then, after a long weekend away from my office, I pick up a voicemail.

"Hi, Dr. Weber. It's Peter. I know I acted badly during my last session, but I did listen to what you said. I'd like to set up another appointment. If you send an email, I will answer it this time."

A week later, Peter walks into my office, well-groomed and dressed in a smart business suit. He smiles and makes eye contact as soon as he sits down. The fidgeting and other signs of anxiety are not in evidence, and he seems relaxed and composed, even happy.

"First, I want to apologize for my outburst the last time I saw you," he begins, with a light tone to his voice that gives him an air of confidence.

"I worried about you," I say.

"I'm sure you did. I was not myself, and I'm afraid I took my anger out on you. Do all of your patients yell at you like I did?"

"No, only the ones I really like!"

Peter smiles from within. I see it in his eyes, hear it in his voice, and feel it from the vibe he's sending out. Looking around, he takes in the familiar surroundings and says, "I want to tell you about the last two months. You pointed out that I was relying too much on my conversations with Jean. I have tried to stop talking to her but I'm only partially successful."

"Tell me what you did."

The smile again surfaces, and Peter seems pleased with himself. "I threw away all of Jean's vitamins and makeup,"

"That's great."

"Not everything is that great. I have hidden some of my feelings and have not been completely open with you about the day of the accident. I need your help."

Peter's face becomes somber and as his smile retreats, hidden creases around his mouth become visible. His eyes deaden.

"Where were you that day?" I ask, hoping I am finding the right key to unlock a door to the inside.

"I was in a conference at work." Peter pauses, looks at his hands, reluctant to continue.

"Was there anything different about that day?"

Peter's mood changes and he becomes upset. He stands up and slowly walks to the window. "Do you mind if I walk around while I talk? It helps me organize my thoughts."

"Go ahead."

"I still have difficulty telling you this part because it is so painful," stammers Peter. His words come out slow with an economy of sentiment, trying to say the right thing with the least amount of energy. With halting speech, he continues, "I got a phone call at work, but I ignored it because I was busy and didn't want to be bothered. An hour later, I listened to the message and my world collapsed."

Peter paces between the window and my desk, hands in his pockets, eyes downcast. The stammering increases, and at times he is inaudible. "It was the hospital calling to tell me my wife had been in an accident, and she wanted to talk to me. No other information. I got to the hospital as quickly as I could, the entire time cursing myself for not picking up the message earlier. In my head, I rehearsed how I was going to explain to Jean that I would never put my job before her needs again."

Peter pauses for a moment as emotions start to overwhelm him. He looks to me for reassurance. Walking back to the comfortable chair, he sits down and appears more composed.

"When I got to the hospital, it was too late. Jean passed away without ever saying goodbye. The pain was intolerable. I left the hospital to gather my sons and the look in their eyes was more than I could bear. We broke into a million pieces."

"It's good that you shared this moment with me," I say.

"I hope you can help me."

"I think I can. I understand these feelings, a sudden death, two young children, and no chance to say goodbye."

"But I could have said goodbye if only I would have answered the phone. What kind of idiot doesn't answer their phone when his wife is in the hospital?"

"Peter, you didn't know Jean was in the hospital." I see pain threading across his face and his guilt is heartbreaking. I give him time to collect himself and say, "I can help you find a way to balance your life so you can honor Jean, but at the same time not rely on her help in making decisions for your boys."

"Is that psychobabble?" he smiles ever so slightly.

"No," I say. "It's something you're going to have to learn."

Both Peter and I take a drink of water to slow down our thinking and create some space after the difficult session. As a therapist, I am invested in Peter and want to see him repair his life. I ask, "How are your boys doing?"

"All right. I had each of them keep a personal item to remind them of their mother. I did the same. It's surprising what each took, since it wasn't what I would have predicted. Brian kept a juice glass because Jean made him smoothies in that glass, and Jeff took the flowerpot he'd decorated for Jean when he was at camp. Following my son's lead, I took a macramé wall hanging Jean made for me as a gift, even though I never really liked it. I still cannot bring myself to clean out her closet because I can't let go of the smell of her clothing."

"This is progress. Let's try to get to the next step. You say you talk to Jean to help you through difficult situations. Have you ever told her how you feel?"

"I only ask for help." Peter is quiet for a moment before he continues. "It's hard for me to talk about that stuff."

"You could try writing a letter to Jean and give yourself the opportunity to say things that are difficult, or you may have left unsaid."

Peter sits unresponsive as he opens and closes his hands on his lap, twisting his wedding band around his fingers. After a long silence, he says, "When you first suggested I clean out all of Jean's personal items, I went ballistic. I'm sure you remember. This next request about writing a letter hits me the same way. I want to go ballistic, but I will give it some thought."

"Good," I say.

"I need some time to think about this. Give me a few weeks and I'll set up another appointment, and we can discuss it again."

"I understand. See you in a few weeks."

After Peter leaves, I look out at the rolling waves of Lake Michigan just beyond my office window. I do my best thinking while staring at their ever-changing movements; it has a calming effect that releases my mind from clutter. I am optimistic about Peter's treatment, but his problem brings up issues within myself that I now question. I'm not sure I ever resolved the guilt I felt from my inattentive behavior during my mother's illness. It has been forty years since her passing, but how long can guilt live within you?

That night after dinner, Billy calls from school to catch up on what's been happening. He sounds good and says that calculus is going better now that he is studying harder.

"How are things with you, Mom?" Billy asks.

"Pretty good," I respond. "You remember that patient I told you about with complicated grief? I saw him today and I think he is on the right path."

"What therapy did you use?"

"I have a lot of special techniques."

"C'mon, Mom, don't be evasive."

"Okay, talking to his dead wife was an issue. He needed closure and I suggested that he write a letter to his wife, telling her how he feels."

"And that works?"

"Maybe. I hope it gives him closure."

"Great. You should try that on yourself."

As I hang up the phone, I think about my sensitive, intuitive son. He is so introspective and sees things from a different angle. I should listen to what he has to say.

Dear Lizzie,

Hi Mom, it's Kim, only forty years late in exploring my emotions and feelings about our time as parent and child. We only had sixteen years together and never knew each other as adults, so I want you to know that I am doing well and am happy in my life. I have a husband who loves me, and we have a son, Billy. Julie's family is also doing well, and we all get together on holidays to celebrate our good fortune.

I am a psychologist with a private practice, and I help

*people deal with their feelings. Now I am trying to help myself.
It is 2001, and we have different ways to describe our emotions.
One of the new terms is "closure" (you may have called it
"peace" or "satisfaction"), and I want closure regarding your
passing. My son suggested I write this letter to you.*

*I was fifteen when cancer struck. At the time, I was
searching for my own identity and trying to establish a sense
of self. My friends were prone to influence my behavior, and
I sometimes got angry when your illness inconvenienced my
social life. How self-centered I was! You were the one who was
facing the loss of life, and yet, I was the one who felt angry. For
that, I am sorry.*

*Looking back on my childhood, I remember you as being
our protector. Dad was strict and often angry, but you never
let Julie or I suffer any of the emotional consequences of his
behavior. Do you remember when I broke a window on my
way to catch the school bus? I was afraid to come home that
afternoon and face Dad, but when I walked up to the door,
you had fixed the window, and the broken glass was never
discussed. I was grateful for your intervention but never
thanked you. I'll say it now. Thank you!*

*Today, chemotherapy is an effective tool for fighting cancer,
but it wasn't available for you. The radiation treatment you
went through would not be as severe today, yet more successful.
I remember picking you up from the hospital each day after
radiation, and you moved so slowly, hesitantly, like you were
about to give in to gravity. I think you already knew that you
were fighting a losing battle.*

*This letter seems to jump around and is somewhat
disorganized. I wanted to let my thoughts just bleed onto the
page so I could really hear what my feelings were telling me.
I'm trying to figure out if I have "complicated grief" (another*

new term), or if I was able to properly resolve my sorrow. Please be patient with my ramblings.

I remember one Friday night in the fall when I went to my high school football game. My boyfriend at the time was a running back on the team, and I was proud to be the girlfriend of a jock (how stupid I was!). However, earlier that day, I had taken you to your doctor's appointment, and you looked devastated upon leaving his office. I knew something was wrong. That night at dinner, Dad told us you had cancer.

I think you always knew that cancer was a possibility, but you never talked about it. We all cried, but Dad insisted I still go to the football game, just like always. I sat in the stands, among my friends, but never saw the game. I sat in silence, thinking about you.

That night changed everything; I realized I was losing you. Everybody helped out, Aunt Ruth took care of you during the day, I had special permission to leave school early so I could drive you to the radiation treatments, even though they turned out to be a wasted effort, and Julie took care of the house. Dad spent his nights with you, and I was surprised to see him so attentive.

Do you remember the gold coin you gave me when you first got sick? You said your father had given it to you when you married Dad, and he carried it during his time in the war. I also carried it with me until I almost lost it during an incident in my hippie days. Fortunately, I found it and put it in a locked safe until yesterday, when I needed to see it.

Opening the safe, I looked at the coin for the first time in many years. The portrait of Lady Liberty was still shiny, and the laurel wreath on the back symbolized triumph, a good feeling for all of us. It was a $1 gold piece but is worth a fortune today. Don't worry, I'll never sell it, because it means *too much to me. I plan to follow your lead and pass it on to my son. I will tell him the history of this talisman.*

When your suffering ended and you passed, there was relief in our family that the ordeal was over. I hope that you never thought any of us ever wanted to live without you, but the process was long, and you suffered enough. Each of us dealt with our grief individually. I'm not sure that grieving alone is the best way to resolve issues, but I didn't know any other way.

I am sorry that we never got to know each other as adults, never got to go places together as friends, and never got to just hang out and talk. We would have been good friends, and happy in each other's company.

When I had a child of my own, I often thought of you and the insane kind of love a parent feels for their child. I knew that is how you felt about Julie and me. You passed too soon but left a legacy that will be here forever.

Love,
Kim

ROUND SIX

KIM

MAY 10, 2009

Mark and I decide that once round six is over, we will switch doctors because we don't feel comfortable with Dr. Belmont. I never doubted his competence, but there is something upsetting about his mannerisms. We decide on an oncologist at University Hospital.

Dr. Caldron walks into the examination room and greets us warmly with a handshake. I immediately like him; his presence exudes charm and confidence. He looks like someone you would trust if you approached him on the street for directions. His smile is friendly and sincere and I did not experience the "white coat" syndrome of other doctor visits. His khaki pants, blue-checkered shirt, and red tie added to the casual feel of gentle intelligence.

After some preliminary questions about the diagnosis and treatment, Dr. Caldron says, "You are in remission."

"How do you know? The lab work isn't even in yet."

"I don't have to look at today's data," Dr. Caldron explains. "You look like a healthy person. Your posture is upright, your color is good, and you smiled while you answered my questions."

I'm happy to have a smile, I say to myself, but I still cannot push away the dark thoughts that live within me. "I only recently got back my smile," I comment, "but you're making me feel good."

"I'd like to think I can magically sense when a person goes into remission," Dr. Caldron says with optimism, the antithesis of the gloomy death prognosis of past doctors. "But other quantifiable factors go into my decisions. You had a strong response to the first round of chemotherapy, which quickly removed a lot of the cancer cells. Not all lymphoma patients do, and most can't tolerate the chemo process as well as you did."

"What is my prognosis?" I ask.

"There is no way of predicting the future, so it is impossible to say for sure. My best advice is to go live your life."

I look at Mark and see joy and relief spread across his face. A release valve opens and tension melts away as his brows relax and his mouth loosens into a broad smile. Even his posture changes. He straightens his spine and lifts his shoulders in a single fluid motion, unlocking the burden of dealing with my illness. This is the information he's been waiting for, but I am less assured and hold back my feelings.

Our ride home takes us through the pastoral beauty of Wisconsin. We pass through rolling landscapes and fields where corn, wheat, and soy will soon begin their growth cycle. Distant farms look like artistic renderings; bucolic settings embrace nature with a mix of colors and a blend of textures. The full spectrum of the rainbow shimmers before us, but I stay in grayscale. Even the gold coin I'm rubbing between my fingers cannot bring light into my world.

Mark is probably thinking everything will be all right, as is typical of his unrealistic optimism. He doesn't know I am still harboring thoughts of death. I am careful to plaster a frozen smile on my face and say the right things, all happiness and bliss. Mark cannot read the darkness below the surface.

He doesn't know that cancer opened a path for me, a road I only travel in my imagination, a road leading me to peace. My cancer is the escape hatch from my constant grief, a way to end my sorrow and find rest. I embrace it. I do not fear it, because I want to be released from the vise holding me in this meaningless existence.

I couldn't tell Mark about those feelings because he lives in denial and overt happiness. It has been more than five years since we lost Billy, but when he died, I wanted to die with him. Mark suffered too, but he was able to tuck the pain into the far recesses of his brain and not acknowledge its existence. Billy's death destroyed our family, our marriage, and my soul.

I still remember the boy with the generous smile, his hugs freely given and accepted by me. He was curious about everything from problems in the universe to how to make his favorite salad dressing. He delighted in surprising me with homemade gifts and sat with Mark on Sundays watching NFL Football. When did the darkness set in? It wasn't there as Billy was growing up. I don't even think it was there when he was away at college. I tell myself I would have seen it, I should have seen it, but I did not. The three a.m. call from the police brought my world to an end and I became an empty person.

"Hello?" Mark wakes up to the shrill ringing of the phone. Any call in the middle of the night signals danger, and both of us become alert.

"Yes, that's me."

Momentary silence as Mark listens to the caller.

"What are you saying? That can't be." Mark's fingers begin to spasm as he grips the phone. In the dim light of the phone, I see panic in his eyes.

"Mark, put it on speaker," I say, knowing something is terribly wrong.

The man on the phone speaks. "I'm sorry to be the one to tell you, but your son Billy has died of a gunshot wound."

"How can that be?" Mark looks toward me. "He lives alone in an apartment in Brooklyn. He wouldn't be out on the streets at this time of night. You must have the wrong person."

"I'm sorry, Mr. Weber. It was a self-inflicted wound."

Disbelief. Time freezes and the air in the room strangles me, halting my breath and shutting down my brain. My bowels churn and bile rises in my throat, sending me running into the bathroom to vomit relentlessly, over and over until there is nothing inside me but emptiness. I splash my face with cold water, thinking this is a horrible dream, but when I hear Mark asking more questions, I lose my balance and topple to the floor. Convulsive crying pulsates in waves of despair.

A distraught Mark comes into the bathroom to check on me, but he is also beyond help. Both of us crouch on the floor in utter grief, knowing at some point we will have to move, but unable to put our bodies in motion. Finally, I ask Mark what else the police officer said, but all he could come up with was that we had to go to Brooklyn to claim the body.

The following weeks are a blur, nothing familiar or right. Following the funeral, Mark and I try to put the pieces of our life together. We talk to Billy's friends, who are also shocked by his suicide, but nobody can offer insight into the why, only that he was stressed from working long hours.

Mark and I go through the motions of living, but our lives have been ripped apart and a growing wedge forms between us. We are alone and hurting, grieving in different ways, but nothing will bring us back to the unit we once called a family.

"We're almost home." Mark's voice interrupts my thoughts. "What do you want to do for dinner tonight?"

"It's been an exhausting day. Let's eat at home."

"It's almost summer," Mark says. "Do you want me to fire up the grill? I think we have some chicken breasts in the refrigerator."

"Good, I'll make a salad."

We are silent for a while before I ask, "Mark, do you remember when I thought my cancer came from something in my background?"

"I do remember. You were convinced you inherited the cancer gene."

"I don't believe that anymore," I say with certainty. "My family is rich in characters but not prone to illnesses. Occasionally, there were incidents of stupidity, even me in my youth, but my family is strong and hardy. My problem is that I think too much, worry too much, and expect too much. It creates stress and I think that is where the cancer started. Stress."

"No one knows for sure," Mark says, turning on to the exit ramp leading home.

Sinking into the car seat, I rub my eyes as I brush away the tears. I am in remission. I should relax, de-stress, get rid of the fatalistic thoughts that haunt me, but instead my muscles remain rigid, my brows furrow, and my neck muscles are tight. Complicated grief follows me past remission and still attacks every part of my being. If only I could take a pill to make it go away, like chemotherapy for grief, but emotions are not data-based and can linger on for an eternity.

I try to meditate. I breathe deeply, close my eyes, and silently chant a repetitive mantra, but it is useless. My mind goes back to our last trip to New York, when I spoke at the symposium about complicated grief. Mark liked the speech; I did not. The topic was too close to my heart, and I was afraid the audience would pick up on my anxiety. How did I expect to get through to a room full of strangers when I was unable to reach into my own feelings?

Once home, we prepare for dinner. The evening is unseasonably warm, so we eat outside on our newly renovated patio. Mark and I designed the area to remind us of our trip to Italy, where we had many pleasant dinners on the verandas of old Italian mansions. Our wrought-iron table sits under a grape arbor covered with young plants that are not fully grown but dense enough to provide shade and seclusion. In every corner, we have large Talavera pots, Toulon planters, and one oversized Campagna Olive Jar filled with soil but not yet planted. Cobblestone pavers replicate the roads of ancient Italy and add to the old-world charm of our small space. It is cozy and welcoming, but I sometimes miss our old red-brick floor covered with moss and lichen and slim wands of grass poking out of the cracks. The echo of bare feet running across those bricks, along with the infectious laughter of children, cannot be replaced by cobblestone pavers.

"How is the chicken?" Mark asks.

"Good," I respond.

In leu of meaningful conversation, we discuss what flowers to buy for our planters, if we need fertilizer, and what to do to keep the chipmunks and squirrels out of our garden. Anything to avoid the obvious conversation we need to have.

Mark asks, "How did you like Dr. Caldron?"

"He was good," I respond, "I'm happy the chemo is over. I can handle a checkup every three months."

"It's great you're in remission. Now we can think about what our future looks like."

"Sure," I say as I clear the table and get ready to go inside.

"What is wrong with you?" Mark asks annoyed with my indifference. "You should be thrilled the cancer is gone, but you're acting like you're disappointed."

I put the dirty dishes down on the side bar next to the door and sigh, tired of this conversation. "You know I am not out of the woods yet. You know there is still uncertainty about the future."

"I know. But I also know we have been given a pass to live our lives normally and go out and enjoy ourselves."

I turn abruptly to face Mark and go back to the table. My hands twitch and a vein in my forehead starts to pulse. Self-control is a finite resource, and I just ran out of mine. "What do you mean, 'normal'? We haven't been normal in years. Not since Billy died."

Mark retreats as soon as Billy's name is spoken. The mask descends. He looks away, licks his lips, and puts his head down, lowering his eyebrows. "Billy's death has nothing to do with your cancer," he says. "We are free to move on and we can get back our lives."

"I'm not sure I want to get back my life."

"What are you talking about? We can do so much. We can travel again, we can see friends, we can explore new restaurants. We will have a life."

"You have no idea," I say. "I don't want any of those things."

"What do you want?"

I look up but cannot focus. The grape arbor above is a blur and my silence is crushing me. I cannot hold these feeling inside any longer. I shout, "I want Billy, I want to be with Billy."

I crumble into my chair and slowly the tears begin to flow, small droplets that at first soak into my shirt, then crescendo into the wail of a distressed child. I am inconsolable.

Mark rushes to me and hugs me with tenderness. "I want Billy, too," he says, but I push him away, not accepting his empathy

"I can never forgive myself." My words fall quickly, opening my personal truth.

"Why do you need forgiveness?"

I wipe the tears away and bring my gaze to focus on a spider inching its way across the table. I think of *Charlotte's Web*, a book I read to Billy so many years ago. Charlotte found a way to save Wilbur, but no one can save me.

Concentrating on the spider slowly creeping under the table, I open my soul, "I never recognized Billy's problem and I should have."

"That is not true," Mark says. "Nobody knew."

"But I should have. I don't want this guilt to live inside me any longer. The cancer needs to take me and ease my sadness."

For a split second, Mark's grief is suspended, replaced by shock. "Is that why you were so withdrawn from me during your treatment? When you spoke of this before, I did not take you seriously."

"Yes, cancer is my exit strategy." I look at Mark with the angry eyes of unspoken pain. "You know about contingencies. You're an actuary. Every situation has an exit strategy. Well, cancer is mine."

"You can't be serious. Death is not an exit strategy. Healing is." Mark's eyes become dark as he moves from empathy to anger. Glaring at me, he continues. "Billy's death wasn't your fault, and you certainly shouldn't feel guilty for it. Billy would be horrified if he thought his actions pushed you down this dark path." Mark's voice loses its power as his vocal cords malfunction. In a hoarse voice, he says, "You loved him, nurtured him, and supported him in every way."

"But not enough. I'm a psychologist. I should have seen the signs—the depression, the hopelessness, his stress. I was blind to his problems."

"You didn't know."

"You don't understand. I should have known. When Billy was born, friends told me I would be a great mother because of my psychological training. Well, they were all wrong. I don't know anything, and I can't forgive myself for my inability to see what was right in front of me. I deserve to die,"

"No, you don't. Don't ever say that." Mark's rage fills the air, and he walks away from me. Reaching the other side of the patio, he turns to look straight into my eyes. "You are the one who doesn't understand." His words come slow, the hoarseness in his voice like rocks grating against each other. "What does all of your training tell you about someone who does not express emotions?"

Without hesitation I say, "It's not good. If you can't express emotions, you can't deal with them."

"That's right, I hid my pain from you. I never talked about Billy because I couldn't talk about Billy. The loss was too much. My lack of support for him drove me into silence and away from you. I need you. I've always needed you, but we became walled off by our own grief and guilt."

Mark looks away again, breaking eye contact. I see sweat beads on his forehead and a muscle twitches involuntarily at the corner of his eye. After a long, uncomfortable silence, he says, "Billy's death is my fault. I knew about his problems and did nothing. The blame is on me."

In an instant, with those words, my life freezes into a single frame of a video, showing only one scene of a movie. I am paralyzed. My heart still beats, but it beats against a chest that is hollow and empty. I do not understand what Mark has just said.

"What?" I say. "You don't know what you're saying. You never suspected Billy was suffering from anything. He was not depressed. His life was perfect. We were both blindsided by his suicide."

"That is what I wanted you to believe. I let you carry the burden. My suffering was internal and I let you assume the blame. I lost both of you."

"No, you are wrong." I walk to the opposite side of the patio and aimlessly start to dig in the soil. I have nothing to plant but putting my hands in the dirt helps ground me.

"What are you doing over there? Didn't you hear what I said?"

"I did, but you are wrong. What makes you think you could have done anything to prevent Billy's death."

Mark inhales deeply and I hear air stuttering in his lungs as he exhales. I continue to pretend I'm gardening as Mark approaches and hugs me. The panic inside of him crosses our boundaries and seeps into me. I am afraid. All my beliefs are being challenged and I feel lost and insecure. We walk back to the table and Mark speaks in a soft voice, slowly enunciating each syllable as he searches my eyes for understanding.

"Two weeks before Billy died, I had dinner with him in Brooklyn. Remember, I had a business meeting in New York?"

"I remember you coming home upset, but I assumed it was the deal going badly."

"The deal did go badly, but that had nothing to do with me being upset. It was my dinner with Billy. I met him at our favorite vegan restaurant on Fifth Avenue in Park Slope.

Everything seemed fine. We talked about his life in New York, mutual friends, and especially the long hours and demands of his job. After the food arrived, something came over him and he appeared nervous and impatient. I thought maybe the smell of the vegan spices gave him an allergic reaction, or he was upset with the waiter, or me. His eyes blurred, and when I said his name, he looked at me as if I was a stranger. I tried to engage him in conversation, but his response was not relevant to my question. He seemed confused. At one point, he got up from the table to walk around but never went anywhere, just around the table and then back. This unusual behavior lasted at least five minutes and then it was gone."

"Did you ask him what happened?"

"I did, but he didn't seem to remember anything. In fact, he had no recollection of anything being different. I asked him where he went, and he said he didn't go anywhere."

"It almost sounds like a fugue state," I say, thinking out loud. "A person loses memory and wanders around not knowing where he is. It's pretty rare."

"When I asked him about it, he said that sometimes he gets confused and loses track of time, usually when he has to work late. He thought it was caused by a lack of sleep."

"Did he have memory loss?" I ask.

"I think so, but I didn't pursue it. He didn't want to talk about it and started to get angry at me. I suggested he see a doctor to rule out anything serious, but he said he was too busy."

"I'm sure he didn't want to worry you."

"If only I would've insisted on a commitment, a follow-up call to be sure he got help, maybe he would still be with us. But I didn't."

Mark looks at me, tears filling his eyes. His sadness travels into my heart and I once again break down into tears of grief. "Why didn't you tell me?"

Moments pass without Mark looking at me. Finally, regret laced within his words, he says, "I forgot about it. He seemed all right when I left, so I did nothing."

I picture my son, suffering but unwilling to do anything about it. For five years, Mark and I searched for answers, blamed ourselves, and never accepted the fact that Billy had serious problems. We grew apart as a couple, distanced ourselves, each trapped in our own suffering which eventually destroyed our marriage.

"Mark," I say, choking on my words. "You know I blamed myself for not recognizing that something was wrong."

Mark turns away from me and remains motionless. In a quiet voice that's sweet but accusatory, he says, "I felt you were the strong one. Your grieving was open. You specialized in it, so I let you assume the responsibility, knowing you were better than I."

I reach a tipping point where my rage burns. "You don't know me at all. I wanted to die, first when Billy died and now because cancer is a good excuse for ending it all. I do not grieve better than you. I'm looking for a way out. I am not strong."

My tears burn as they pour down my cheeks. I'm shattered. My body feels like an avalanche rolled over it and I am buried with no chance of rescue. Mark thinks I'm solid, able to deal with grief. He is wrong. I want to feel whole again, but I fear all is lost.

Slumping in his chair, Mark takes a sip from the half-full glass of wine. He watches the spider, now on top of the table, and I focus on our grape vines reaching for the sun. We sit in silence as we search for understanding. The emptiness around us is heart wrenching.

After a time, Mark gets up and approaches me cautiously, uncertain of my reaction. He gathers me in his arms with a hug that has enough energy to penetrate my soul. I feel the tenderness of his touch but cannot bear this intimacy. I hit, I yell, I scream, my nose runs, my limbs shake, the hurricane within me rages and I am out of control. Mark continues to hold me, pulling me into his vortex and I finally surrender.

The only sound around us is the silence of agony. I look at Mark through blurry eyes and see that the mask hiding his feelings is gone. There is a softness to his appearance that touches me, a warmth married with understanding. Processing so much pain has brought us to a point of unconditional love and my anger dissipates.

Mark takes my hand as we walk into our house. His physical touch triggers in me the response of the phoenix and I can once again spread my wings and fly. I feel myself healing.

We go to our study, a place we have spent so many years reading, working, and relaxing. Family pictures line the shelves and remind us of the warmth of a family. I walk to the antique desk my grandfather gave to us and open the drawer. My gold coin is in the back corner, and I hold it one more time.

"Four generations of my family owned this coin. I began my search for answers by using its history to find a reason for my illness but ended up finding something more valuable. I found my life."

Mark smiles at me and takes a long look at the coin. "You come from a heritage of strong individuals. Not everybody was perfect, and many of them experienced tragedies, but they survive. You are just like them."

"I wanted Billy to have this coin," I say. "I thought the family legacy, good or bad, would continue with him. That will never happen."

"The legacy is yours," Mark says. "I think it has been good luck despite our tragedies. You have survived and now it is time to embrace the future. Billy cannot give you the peace you want, but we can find it together."

I stare at Mark and somehow feel Billy's presence in the room. The past is still with us, but I have choices to make. I choose Mark, I choose my marriage, I choose good memories of Billy, but most of all, I choose life. The painful memories will never go away, but we will keep them on one side of our brain while holding the good memories on the other side. We will find an interface between the two so we can navigate our new world. Our legacy is love.

I take out a pen and begin to write:

Our Dearest Billy,

ABOUT THE AUTHOR

Karen Shapiro is a retired psychologist with a BA in Education and an MS in Educational Psychology. She also has a certification in graphics and web design. Karen began writing after her sister, an expert in genealogy, found fascinating stories about their ancestors, and she wanted to bring the stories to life through fiction.

Aside from writing, Karen enjoys hiking, yoga, and spending time with her husband, children, and seven grand-mammals—five humans and two dogs.

A NOTE FROM THE AUTHOR

In the time of COVID, it is difficult for an author to do face-to-face events with readers. Word-of-mouth is crucial to my success and if you like *A Shattered Life*, please leave an online review. It will be greatly appreciated.